# DINNER AND A MURDER

### The 3rd Nikki Hunter Mystery

## Nancy Skopin

*This book is for Juliann Stark, my friend, my editor, and my muse, without whom I would be lost.*

*My thanks, once again, to Detective Mark Pollio for his invaluable consultation regarding all matters Police related. Any mistakes herein are my own.*

# PROLOGUE

O N THE MORNING OF HIS *death Gordon Mayes was driving home from work, munching on an organic carrot, and listening to a Jeff Beck CD. He had the volume cranked up and the driver's side window of his SUV open to the chill morning air in an effort to stay alert. It had been a long night.*

*Gordon was an air traffic controller, currently working at San Francisco International. He lived in a two-bedroom condo 45 minutes away in Fremont and drove his Ford Explorer over the San Mateo Bridge to and from work. Even after six months on the graveyard shift Gordon's body clock hadn't adjusted, but at least he beat the rush hour traffic. Gordon prided himself on his ability to see the bright side of almost any situation.*

*Thirty-four years old, divorced with no*

*children, five-ten, and a hundred and seventy-five pounds, Gordon had blond hair, blue eyes, and a dusting of freckles across the bridge of his nose. He worked out regularly, ate a healthy diet, and tried to get eight hours of sleep every day.*

*Gordon enjoyed being an air traffic controller, most of the time. There had only been one major accident while he was on duty, but it had been a terrible disaster and everyone on board had perished. Though he knew he'd done everything possible to save those people, he still carried a deep sense of remorse over their deaths.*

*As he took the exit from Highway 101 onto Highway 92 he glanced over his shoulder and spotted a black Hummer coming up fast. He slowed down to allow the other vehicle to pass before merging into the sparse traffic. Gordon was a considerate driver. Instead of passing him on the left, the enormous vehicle slowed until it was parallel to his Explorer. Gordon looked over, a little nervous because he was running out of on-ramp and getting dangerously close to the low concrete retaining wall on his right. He slowed to twenty miles per hour, and the Hummer matched his speed. Gordon watched as its passenger side window was lowered, and caught a brief glimpse of a dark reptilian shape suspended from the driver's hand before the serpent was hurled through his own open window.*

*The snake brushed Gordon's chin and landed between his legs. He hit the brakes and spun the wheel to the right, instinctively avoiding a collision with the other vehicle. The Explorer crashed into the retaining wall with just enough force to send it over the top. Gordon had a momentary sense of weightlessness as the SUV flipped and plummeted to the deserted street below. It landed upside down, killing Gordon almost instantly.*

*The driver of the Hummer took the Delaware exit and drove along side streets until he was half a block from the ruined Explorer. He waited patiently, watching for signs of life.*

# CHAPTER 1

**M**Y NAME IS NICOLI HUNTER. I'm a Private Investigator licensed to practice in California. My office is in Redwood City in a marina complex where I also live aboard my forty-six foot sailboat, *Turning Point*. I've been living aboard since I got divorced, earned my PI license, and opened my own office just over two years ago.

Most of my customers are bar and restaurant owners who hire me to conduct covert employee surveillance. However, in the last few months I've handled two murder investigations during which I brushed up against the Grim Reaper, so lately I've appreciated the simple things in life more than I used to. For this reason alone, when an invitation to my high school reunion arrived in the mail, it appealed to me. I optimistically filled out the enclosed questionnaire.

> *1. What is your current occupation?*
> Private Investigator
>
> *2. What is your spouse or significant other's name and occupation?*
> Occasional significant other: Bill Anderson, Police Detective
>
> *3. What are the names and genders of your children?*
> Not Applicable
>
> *4. Where are you currently living?*
> Aboard my sailboat in Redwood City, California

I finished filling out the form and was enclosing a check when I developed cold feet, remembering why I had chosen to avoid all of the previous reunions. I'd had a miserable time in high school. It never made sense to me that I was required to attend classes when I had better things to do, and I was not one of the popular kids. I was creative and eccentric, hanging out with the big-brains, drama geeks, and stoners, who also didn't fit in.

Suddenly undecided about this upcoming event, I called my best friend, Elizabeth Gaultier. Elizabeth also lives aboard, on a trawler docked at the base of the companionway not far from my boat, which is how we met. She answered on the second ring.

"Hi, honey. What's up?" Elizabeth has caller ID, but refuses to own a cell phone. She's complicated.

"I'm trying to decide if I want to go to my high school reunion."

Elizabeth knew I'd hated high school, but was quick to remind me that I'd had a few good friends I hadn't seen in years who might attend the reunion, not to mention a few old enemies who should see how good I looked now and how successful I'd become. I thought about that. I'm five-seven and currently a hundred and thirty-eight pounds. I quit smoking a few weeks ago, so I've gained a little weight, but I still fit into my skinny-jeans. I work out five or six days a week and I try to live on the Zone diet. My hair is long, curly, and chestnut brown, and I wear it in a graduated layer cut. My eyes are dark blue with black rims around the irises. I may not be a beauty queen, but I have a good face, apart from the gun powder stippling on my temple from a recent near miss with a homicidal maniac.

"And you could invite Bill along," Elizabeth suggested. "For moral support, *and* to make your old frenemies jealous,"

"What the hell," I said. "If it's a disaster we can leave early."

Thus it was that on a balmy Friday evening in October, I found myself at the Crowne Plaza Hotel in Burlingame where the El Camino High School reunion was being held. Bill had readily agreed to come along. He had never attended one of his own class reunions, so he didn't know what he was getting himself into any more than I did.

Bill is thirty-seven years old, almost six feet tall, lean and well-muscled, with a radiant smile, black hair, hazel eyes, and a dark complexion he inherited from the Lakota Sioux on his mother's side. He's definitely eye candy, and I was not above flaunting him in front of my former classmates even if we weren't in a committed relationship.

We arrived late and entered the hotel through a side door because Bill refuses to allow valets to park his classic Mustang. He insists it's because the transmission is temperamental, but I know the truth. A man's car is like his woman. He doesn't want another man to touch her unless she needs medical attention. I know how he feels. I drive a vintage

1972 British racing green BMW model 2002, and every time I drop it off at Bimmers in San Carlos for repairs I get heart palpitations. Not because I don't trust Franjo and Milenko, they're the best BMW mechanics in the State, but whenever I'm without my sweet little 2002 I suffer from feelings of apprehension and distress. I'd recently had the car repainted after it was vandalized by a murderous psycho who was stalking me, so now I'm even more careful about where I park.

We were headed for the front desk to ask where the reunion event was being held when I spotted a ladies' restroom and decided I needed a quick stop. I dashed inside, annoyed by the butterflies in my stomach. I examined my face and hair in the mirror, added lip gloss, and then selected a stall. I was seated when I heard the restroom door open and a group of women enter, all talking at once. I didn't recognize any of the slightly tipsy voices until I heard one woman call another by name.

"You haven't changed a bit, Cher," said the voice.

"Oh my God!" I blurted out. "Is that Cher Costanza?"

"Yes," sang a familiar blonde voice. "Who's that?"

"It's Nikki Hunter!" I quickly stood and

pulled up my bikini briefs as the automatic
commode flushed itself. I was wearing my
favorite little black halter dress with my Stuart
Weitzman peep-toe pumps. This was extremely
formal attire for me. I spend most of my life in
shorts or jeans.

I opened the stall door and time flew back
nineteen years as I gazed into the face of my
best high school buddy. I'd skipped a grade
and graduated at seventeen, so, at thirty-seven,
Cher had a year on me. The fact that we hadn't
stayed in touch didn't stop us from instantly
reverting to the teenagers we used to be. We
quickly hugged, then stood back and examined
each other, simultaneously announcing, "You
look great!" and bursting into fits of laughter.

Bill, waiting outside in the hallway,
must have thought there was a cheerleader's
convention taking place in the ladies' restroom.

Cher had changed so little that I was
stunned. She still had the same shoulder-
length blonde hair with bangs cut a little long.
She had to tilt her chin up slightly in order to
see out from under them. She was tan, even in
October, and wore the same black eyeliner and
pink lipstick I remembered so well, though a
bit more skillfully applied than it had been in
high school. Her figure was still trim and she
was wearing a Versace Graffiti Print dress with

a very short skirt. In fact it was so short that she might be arrested for indecent exposure if she bent over in public, but it totally worked on her. Her cerise-pink polished toes peeked out of a pair of nude Manolo Blahnik ankle strap sandals that added four inches to her height.

Cher and I smoked our first cigarettes together in the El Camino High girls' restroom during lunch. Salems. I wondered if she still smoked. I couldn't smell tobacco on her, but you can't always tell. Besides, she was wearing Flowerbomb, a floral scent that would mask almost anything.

When I got over the shock of seeing her again, I turned to see who Cher had been talking to. I was met with polite smiles from Heather Crossgill and Melissa Hutchinson— two of my former arch-enemies. They both looked fit, but they were dressed like fifty-dollar hookers. Cher always had a kind of innate elegance, even in high school when her wardrobe was tacky. In addition to the innate grace with which she carries herself, I attribute this to her angelic disposition. Heather and Melissa, on the other hand, were mean-spirited, petty, back-biting, two-faced bitches who wouldn't give me and Cher the time of day back in high school. I couldn't help but wonder why they were hanging on her every word now. Surely they hadn't changed. The mean girls in high school grow up to become mean women, don't they?

When I looked back at Cher I noted the huge diamond on her ring finger and the one carat studs in her ears. Combined with the Versace and Manolos, the look shouted opulence. So *that* was it. Heather and Melissa were drawn to Cher now because she had money. I was halfway through this ugly thought when it dawned on me that I had traveled, emotionally, back to our ninth grade gym class when Heather and Melissa had made fun of me because my bra didn't match my panties, or maybe it was because my panties didn't match my bra. The point is, I tend to hold a grudge.

"Hi guys. How are you?" I said, smiling at my old adversaries.

"Is that gorgeous hunk of man waiting outside your husband?" Heather stage whispered.

"He's mine all right," I said. Let there be no mistake about that. "But we aren't married." I felt my smile grow frosty as I hastily rinsed my hands.

"So where's our venue?" I asked, hoping to shift the topic away from Bill and defuse the childish surge of jealousy I was feeling.

"Come on, I'll show you. We just stepped out
to grab a drink at the bar. There's no bar in
our banquet room. Can you believe that?"

She grabbed my arm and we exited the
restroom together, with Heather and Melissa
trailing behind.

I introduced Bill to all three women and,
being a perfect gentleman, he shook hands with
each of them. Steam started coming out of my
ears when Heather held onto Bill's hand with
both of hers for what felt like a full minute. He
must have known I was contemplating a body
slam because he flicked me a glance that said
*chill*. As soon as Heather released him, Bill put
his arm around my shoulder and kissed me,
scoring major points to be cashed in later in
the evening. He kept his arm around me as
Cher led the way across the lobby to the room
where the reunion was being held, Heather
and Melissa weaving along behind us.

While Bill and I got in line to register,
Cher said she would find our place markers
and move them to her table.

The registration area was manned by
Arabella Tribuzio, at least that had been her
maiden name. Her nametag read Bella Piazza.
Unlike Cher, Bella had changed. She looked
her age, but had somehow grown into her

eyes, nose, and teeth. In high school all three had seemed too large for her face. Now she just looked dramatic.

When we finally made it to the front of the line Bella looked up at Bill, smiled broadly, and then turned her attention to me. Her mouth dropped open and her eyes widened. "Well I'll be damned," she said. "When they told me you were coming I said, *'I don't believe it,'* but here you *are!* Nikki Hunter. How the hell are you? Where have you been for the last nineteen years, and who is *this* handsome devil?" She waggled her eyebrows at Bill.

It was Bella all right. She always said what was on her mind. I'd liked that about her.

"This is Bill Anderson," I said. "I'm doing well. I live in Redwood City now, and I'm a private investigator. Does that cover everything?" I was smiling when I said this, and you have to know Bella. She's over-the-top, Italian, and not easily offended.

She was checking our names off on her list and before she could respond someone behind us said, "Can we keep the line moving?"

I spun around, ready to bite off the head of the jerk who was rude enough to rush me at my first reunion, when I did one of those ridiculous-looking double-takes. The person standing behind me, grinning ear-to-ear, was none other than Steve Saxon, one of my old high school friends. Steve had been a sensitive kid, which made him a prime target for the jocks, or anyone else who needed to make someone feel small in order to feel good about themselves. He had been the best friend of Sandra Knudson, with whom I attended drama and dance classes, and I'd gotten to know him by association with Sandra. My memories were coming back in a flood.

Steve had aged well. He was over six feet tall, his hair was dark blond, and he'd grown a beard, which completely transformed his appearance. His sparkling blue eyes had the requisite crow's feet and he was dressed in jeans, a turtleneck, and a tweed blazer. If I hadn't been so happy with Bill at the moment I might have made a pass. Instead, I gave Steve a quick hug and introduced him to Bill.

"What have you been up to?" I asked him, as we drifted into the banquet room after Bella had checked him off her list.

The volume of conversation made it hard for me to hear myself, let alone Steve's response.

"I'm living in Maine," he said, managing to scan the room and maintain eye contact with me at the same time. "I'm an artist. Pretty well known in some circles."

"Really?" I didn't remember Steve being

artistic, but I had probably forgotten more about that time than I realized. "What's your medium?"

"Oils, mostly. I dabble in watercolor."

"Subject matter?" I asked.

"Naked women," he said, his eyes flashing.

I looked over at Bill to see if he was paying attention. Regrettably, he was.

"Seriously," I said.

"Seascapes. When I get bored with them I sometimes persuade a lady-friend to pose nude for me. I keep those for my private collection." Steve's eyes made the unspoken suggestion that I look him up if I was ever in Maine long enough for a casual fling. I looked around the room, suddenly anxious to find Cher and our table. I spotted her waving madly from the opposite side of the dance floor.

"Great to see you again, Steve," I said, nudging Bill in the other direction.

"Great to see *you*!" he responded. "Save me a dance."

So, one of my favorite high school friends now fancied himself a ladies' man and was no longer sensitive enough to care that I was here with someone else. I decided it was a minor offence and that I should be flattered, not to mention the fact that I found the way my body was responding to Steve's interest a little disturbing.

Bill and I crossed the room and seated ourselves at Cher's table. She had arranged the place cards so that I was next to her, and Bill was between me and Melissa. Clever girl. She had known that if she seated Bill next to Heather I wouldn't be able to focus on anything else all night. I admit to being the jealous type. I'm territorial and competitive, but until this reunion I'd thought I had those impulses pretty much under control. It seemed my level of maturity had temporarily regressed back to high school.

Once we were seated I noticed Cher's Flowerbomb competing with Heather and Melissa's equally strong and flowery fragrances, and I was glad I'd forgotten to spritz on my own signature scent, Must de Cartier, in my haste to dress for the evening. The fragrances already mingling at our table were enough to make me hurl.

I rested my hand on Bill's thigh and scanned the room for familiar faces. I spotted Sandra Knudson near the entryway. She was talking to a man with a neatly trimmed beard and a receding hairline dressed in jeans and a brown leather bomber jacket. He looked familiar. I stared at him for a minute, but couldn't quite place him. Then I looked away and it hit me. Paul Marks! Paul and I had walked to school together for more years than I could remember. He'd lived around the corner from my house and had taken piano lessons from my mom. Adorable, sweet, loyal Paul Marks. We'd been hot and heavy for a while in high school, before deciding we were better off as friends.

I waved and both Paul and Sandra waved back. Why hadn't I stayed in touch with these people? A moment later Paul strode over to our table and knelt beside my chair as I turned to greet him.

"Nikki," he said, reaching for my hand. "I can't believe you finally came to one of these things. I thought I'd never see you again. You look beautiful." He gave my hand a quick squeeze and leaned in for a kiss on the cheek.

Paul always had intense brown eyes with long lashes and an aura of kindness, and that hadn't changed. I felt my heart swell with affection, but I also noticed his face was thinner now, almost gaunt. I supposed it could be part of the natural aging process, but it didn't look healthy on him. Although he was smiling, I could sense anxiety just beneath the surface.

I introduced Paul to Bill and they shook

19

hands, maintaining eye contact long enough to tell me that Bill was feeling a little bit territorial himself tonight. The moment was slightly awkward, but not unpleasant.

"So, Paul," I said, "What have you been up to for the last nineteen years?" That sounded lame even to me, but I was genuinely interested.

"I'm an air traffic control supervisor at SFO," he said. "Recently promoted. I've been married once. No kids. We're divorced now. What about you?"

All right, I thought, such a high-pressure job could easily account for the level of stress Paul exhibited.

I smiled and said, "I'm a private investigator. I live aboard a sailboat in Redwood City."

That was the condensed version, but the room was too noisy for a conversation about how many times I'd been married and the career path that led me to my current occupation. I pulled a business card out of my purse and handed it to him. He studied it for a minute, frowning slightly, then fished a card out of his wallet.

"Let's have lunch," he said.

I nodded enthusiastically. "I'd like that."

A moment later Paul left to find his own table.

While we'd been talking the waitstaff had

begun pouring ice water and were now serving green salads liberally doused with bright orange dressing. I placed my napkin on my lap, picked up my fork, and looked around the banquet room, listening to the idle chatter at surrounding tables and the clink of silverware. The lighting in the room was dim, but I could see that there were four long tables set up against the back wall, covered with works of art, articles of clothing, and gift baskets. I couldn't for the life of me figure out what that was about.

I turned to Cher. "What's all the merchandise for?" I asked pointing toward the back of the room.

She laughed and leaned against me saying, "It's a silent auction. Proceeds go to the school. This isn't just a reunion, it's a fundraiser."

I'd never been to a reunion and I'd never been to a silent auction, so I was totally clueless. Good thing I had a guide. I noticed Cher was ignoring her salad too, so I asked if she wanted to go take a look at the auction tables.

"Yes," she answered quickly.

I asked Bill if he wanted to join us, but he took a pass. I kissed him on the lips and glanced across the table at Heather, who gave me a snide grin. I really wanted to slap her. Sometimes I hate being human.

# CHAPTER 2

CHER AND I STROLLED ARM-IN-ARM toward
the back of the room. The first table
was loaded with alluring baskets of beauty
products. Cher picked up an auction sheet for
one of them, and I read over her shoulder. It
showed a minimum bid of thirty dollars. She
added her name and a bid of thirty-one dollars.

Among the items on the next table was a
small oil painting of a coastline that looked
like it might be in Maine. I leaned in close to
the canvas and read the signature. Steve Saxon.
The technique was slightly impressionistic but
the painting was not lacking in detail and
displayed no small amount of talent. I read the
minimum bid on the auction sheet, and caught
my breath. This tiny, unframed work of art was
listed for a minimum of a thousand dollars.
It was good, but was it that good? I guess it

depends on the size of your wallet. There were already three bids on the sheet. Melissa had bid one thousand and fifty dollars, Sandra had bid a thousand seventy-five, and Heather had bid fifteen hundred. I wondered what Heather thought she was buying. I know, *meow*.

I looked over at Cher who was examining a handmade jacket designed by Bella's cousin Pete. I remembered him and wasn't surprised he'd gone into fashion. It was a black and tan wool blazer, and it was elegant. The minimum bid was a hundred dollars, which was a steal. I was tempted, but I already owned a blazer, and when you live on a boat you learn to minimize. I did add my bid for a "Super Lucky Dog" tee shirt, also designed by Pete. It was a patchwork of color with a large red "S" in the middle of a royal blue triangle on the chest. You can never have too many tee shirts, and this one was charming.

The next item on the table was a harlequin doll with porcelain face, hands, and feet. The minimum bid was forty-five dollars. Cher listed her name on that sheet as well, for forty-six. I glanced at the diamond wedding set on her left hand and wondered if her husband could afford a rock that size because she was such an adept bargain hunter.

"Tell me about your life," I said. "I want

to know everything that's happened since I last saw you. Don't leave anything out."

Cher put her arm around me and gave me a squeeze. "I'm sorry I didn't stay in touch. I guess I was in such a hurry to brush South City off my shoes that I left the good things behind with the bad."

"Now you're making me feel guilty," I said. "I didn't stay in touch with you either."

"We're even, then" she said. "I guess you know I went to Columbia as a Lit major, since that was the plan I hatched before graduation. What you don't know is that I was only there for six months before I met Mister Right." She grimaced as she said this. "His name was Hal Stoakes, and he was tall, dark, handsome, intelligent, sexy, and well-off. We dated for three years and when he proposed I didn't hesitate." She paused for a moment, gazing off into space. "Have you been married, Nikki?" She turned to look at me.

"Three times," I cringed. "The first was during our senior year, remember?"

That got a laugh out of Cher. "Oh my God, that's right! You always were the wild one. You'll know what I mean then. People change when they get married. It's like something that's been hiding deep inside crawls out and bites you on the ass."

She was somber. Not something I would have believed her capable of in high school.

"Is your marriage in trouble?" I asked. I couldn't believe how quickly the bond between us had been reestablished. I hadn't seen this woman since I was seventeen, yet I was ready to do battle to ensure her happiness. I'm really a knight in PI's clothing. If I don't watch it, I get myself into all kinds of trouble trying to protect the people I care about, and sometimes people I don't even know. I attribute this to my inability to defend myself as a child when I was victimized by my cousin Aaron.

Cher reached for my hand. "I guess it has been for years. But let's not talk about that tonight. Let's just have fun and get reacquainted. We can get together later to discuss what's wrong with my life and how to fix it."

The warm feeling I'd had at seeing Cher again became melancholy as I envisioned her trapped in a loveless marriage.

After dinner we all crowded onto the dance floor for a group picture, then a disk jockey began playing music that had been popular when we were teenagers. I liked some of the old songs, but I didn't like the memories most of them evoked. I watched Steve Saxon dancing with Sandra Knudson. They moved so well together it was impossible to imagine they had never been a couple. I hoped Steve wouldn't approach me for a dance. No way could I keep up with his moves.

When the song ended I saw Steve glance in my direction, and I hastily dragged Bill out of his chair and toward the dance floor. Bill does *not* like to dance. Although he's naturally graceful he seems to think that *real men* don't dance, and it makes him feel foolish. Thankfully, the song the disk jockey had selected was a slow one. I inhaled the subtle scent of Grey Flannel as I leaned my head against Bill's shoulder. He was a saint for coming to this reunion with me, and dancing just added more points to the roster. I hoped that if the time ever came for me to return the favor, I would be half as gracious.

My reverie was broken when I glanced across the room and saw Paul suddenly reach in his jacket and pull out his iPhone. He was too far away and there were too many people between us, for me to hear what he said, but I could see that the call disturbed him. He seemed to curl in on himself as he dropped his head before returning the phone to his pocket. Dancers moved in front of him then, and I couldn't see him, but moments later he appeared at my side.

"Excuse me, I'm sorry," Paul said, nodding to Bill, who stepped back. He looked pale, almost white, and his face was more drawn than ever. "When I said we should have lunch, Nikki, I was just happy to see you again and wanted to get together. But something has come up and I'd like to meet with you as soon as possible. Could we have lunch tomorrow?"

"Of course," I said, trying not to let him see how concerned I was. "Call me at the office in the morning. I'll rearrange my schedule if I need to." I gave him a quick hug, which he returned before bolting from the room.

"What the hell was that about?" Bill asked.

"No idea," I said, leaning back into his arms, now worried about both of my old friends.

When the music stopped, Bella appeared on the dance floor with one of those cordless microphones and said it was time to announce the silent auction winners. She made it sound like a contest, and I guess in a way it was. Cher won both items she had bid on and smiled contentedly as she wrote out the check. Heather won Steve's painting for fifteen hundred dollars. There was a toxic gleam in her eyes when she gave Bella her check and received the prized work of art.

After all the auction items had been

awarded Bella made a huge production of thanking the individuals who had donated them. She asked each contributor to come out on the dance floor one at a time, and the crowd applauded politely for each of them. When Steve Saxon stepped up the applause was deafening and there were a few decidedly feminine catcalls and whistles. There may not have been a bar in our banquet room, but there were several in the hotel, and some of my classmates had apparently paid them more than one visit.

The whole reunion experience was surreal for me. Apart from meeting up with Cher and Paul again, I think I could have done without it. I knew I wouldn't rest well until I found out what was troubling Paul, but seeing the two of them made the whole thing worthwhile.

At the end of the evening Cher and I exchanged numbers and made a lunch date for the following weekend, promising to touch base before then to discuss where and when. She was living in Burlingame now, only twenty minutes away from the marina. I'd probably invite her to The Diving Pelican so I could give her a tour of my office and my boat.

As Bill and I were walking through the lobby on our way out I spotted Steve and Heather sitting next to a huge potted palm, talking intently. Heather had one hand on Steven's leg and a cocktail in the other. They both looked up as we passed by. I waved and kept Bill moving toward the exit.

Once we were on the freeway headed home I said, "That was weird."

"What?" Bill asked, dutifully.

"Being around all those people I haven't seen in nineteen years."

"You seemed to have a good time," he offered.

"I did, I guess. It's great to be back in touch with Cher. We had some wild times when we were teenagers. And Paul is so sweet. I'm glad I went. But I don't think I ever want to do it again."

"Sweet, huh?"

He was grinning, and normally isn't the jealous type. Nevertheless, I felt the need to defend myself. "Yes, sweet. There hasn't been anything romantic between us since high school, and there certainly isn't now. He's just a good person. You know, true blue, salt of the earth. Stop me before I cliché again."

"Okay. I get the idea."

# CHAPTER 3

BILL AND I HAD ARRIVED back at the
Marina and were walking down the
companionway to the dock when I had an
impulse to stop and knock on the door of
Elizabeth's trawler. I needed a reality check,
but it was late and her lights were off. I
decided I could wait until morning to bend
her ear about my reunion experience.

Elizabeth is my sounding board when I
can't figure out what's right in front of me.
She's a strawberry blonde pixie about five feet
tall with a genius level IQ, and my closest
female friend. I wanted to share everything
that had happened tonight with her. I needed
to decompress by telling her about the people
I hadn't seen for so long, but wished I'd stayed
in touch with, and the people who had been
assholes in high school and apparently still

were. I wanted to hear what she would say about my lusting after Steve, even though I was in a 'relationship' with Bill. I knew Elizabeth would be able to put everything in perspective. I'd have to invite myself over tomorrow for an early morning chat.

We continued down the dock to my boat, where we shucked off our clothes and crawled into the queen-size bunk with a minimum of conversation. Once we were in bed Bill rolled onto his side and pulled me close, copping a feel and nuzzling my neck, then promptly began snoring. This is one of his gifts. No matter what's going on in his life, no matter how disconcerting the cases he's working on may be, he can always sleep.

I am of the opposite variety, an almost chronic insomniac. I only sleep soundly when everything in my life is running smoothly. If anything is amiss, I'm awake. I don't know how to disconnect. I've tried herbs and vitamins and the usual over-the-counter remedies, but nothing seems to work. I even went to a therapist once. Her name was Loretta Dario, and Bill had suggested I talk with her about my reaction to taking a life. He had been right. Even though I'd killed in self-defense, the psychological impact was devastating, and I'd had a *lot* of sleepless nights.

What I really wanted as I lay in bed next to my snoring lover, replaying every minute of the evening, was a cigarette. Because quitting had been such a difficult process for me, as long as I remembered how hard it was I probably wouldn't smoke again. The trouble would begin when I reached the point where I no longer recalled the ordeal of quitting. Then the temptation might get the best of me.

I picked up Michael Connelly's last Harry Bosch novel and read until my eyes would no longer focus. I finally drifted off, and dreamt that something was burning. The smell was so strong in my dream that it woke me. I sat up in bed sniffing the air like a hound who's lost the scent of her prey. The clock said it was 5:13, and Bill was still snoring softly by my side.

A couple of my neighbors have wood stoves onboard their boats, but now that I was awake, the smell was no longer evident. Still, the dream had alarmed me enough that I didn't trust my senses, so I climbed out of bed, careful not to wake Bill, and walked through each of my rooms, sniffing and checking electrical outlets. When I was satisfied that nothing onboard was burning, I pulled on a robe and climbed up into the pilothouse, opened the outer door, and breathed in the cool morning air. Nothing was burning outside either. I was too agitated to attempt sleep again, so I sat down in the pilothouse and waited for sunrise.

I must have fallen asleep, because around 8:00 I was awakened by the scent of coffee, fried eggs, and bacon. Bill can eat whatever he wants without any negative consequences. If I eat anything fried I have to add an hour to my workout. This doesn't stop me from sneaking an occasional strip of bacon off of his plate, however. I stood, stretched, and backed down the companionway into the galley.

Bill gave me a lopsided smile. "You're sleeping in the pilothouse now?"

"Don't look so amused. I thought I smelled smoke and got up to check all the outlets. Then I was too nervous to sleep, so I stayed up to watch the sunrise. Can I have some of your bacon?"

"Help yourself. Just don't blame me when you get on the scale."

Bill isn't insensitive, but he is candid. I actually appreciate that because it means I don't have to waste time wondering about the hidden meaning behind his words. He's got his flaws, of course. He can be critical when it comes to my work. We spend a lot of time arguing about the risks I take, the gray area of the law I tread into when I feel it's necessary, and the fact that he's a little too by-the-book for my taste. Luckily I'm not looking for the perfect man. I'm happy to have Bill in my life whenever we both have time to spend together, and I know he'll be there for me in a pinch. He's had my back on more than one occasion.

After breakfast and a shower I left him onboard noodling on his acoustic guitar, and walked to Elizabeth's trawler. I knocked on the closed door, but there was no response. The fact that the door was closed should have tipped me off. When Elizabeth is at home and awake, her door is usually open, even in cold weather. She'd probably spent the night with Jack at his estate in Hillsborough.

Jack McGuire, retired cat burglar and current inamorata of my best friend, is a former client of mine. I took his case because he was too interesting to turn away. Jack is a red-headed Irishman with the face of a feline. He's playful, witty, charismatic, and gorgeous. I'd inadvertently introduced him to Elizabeth last August when I was working on his investigation.

I hiked up the companionway from Elizabeth's boat, and unlocked my office. The voicemail light was blinking, telling me I had two messages. I started a pot of coffee and turned on my laptop before pushing the play button. The first message was from Paul. It had been left at 1:00 a.m. this morning.

"Hi, Nikki. It was great seeing you tonight and I'm looking forward to lunch. I'm free whenever you are. Call me back?"

In spite of the cheerful words, his voice radiated tension. He left his home number and I made a note of it.

The second message was from the owner of Michelino's in San Mateo, who suspected one of his waitresses was till-tapping. He wanted me to conduct a lunchtime surveillance as soon as possible. The waitress in question worked on Saturdays, so she'd be there today. I don't believe in coincidence, nor do I object when the universe conspires to buy me and a friend lunch. I called Paul's number and the phone rang only once before he answered.

"This is Paul."

"Hey, Paul, it's Nikki. I just got your voicemail. I have to do an employee surveillance job at Michelino's this afternoon, and I was hoping we could meet there for lunch. Will that work for you?"

"Absolutely."

We agreed to meet at 1:00. I made sure Paul knew how to find the restaurant, and ended the call.

For the remainder of the morning I

drank coffee, answered e-mails, and read pre-employment backgrounds I'd requested for one of my clients. I finished up at the office around 12:00 and walked down to the boat to change clothes before meeting Paul. On my way past Elizabeth's trawler I noticed her door was still closed. I wondered if she and Jack were nearing the next level in their relationship, which might mean she'd be moving in with him. For selfish reasons I hoped they weren't. I'd really miss having her so close. Jack's estate is only a fifteen-minute drive from the marina, and there's always the telephone, but it's not the same. It's so much more intimate when you can just drop in and talk with someone in person. I didn't want to lose that.

D'Artagnon, a black Labrador Retriever and self-appointed marina watchdog, was out on the deck of his human's Bluewater 42, so I stopped to scratch behind his ears. D'Artagnon risked his life saving mine a few months ago. We take long walks in the wildlife refuge across the street when weather permits, and he frequently pays me late night visits looking for affection and leftovers. He's only six years old but recently started showing signs of arthritis in his hips and knees. In spite of that, he always enjoys a good romp.

I continued down the dock. As I

approached my boat I heard the resonant tones of Bill's guitar. He was sitting in the main salon with a couple of portholes open, playing one of his original compositions. I stopped for a moment, absorbing the music. Bill has been playing since he was twelve, and he's developed the rare ability to express emotion through his instrument. I could feel each note and the music warmed my heart as it always does when I listen to him play. Eventually I climbed aboard.

"Hey, babe," he called out.

"Hey," I responded. Sometimes you don't need a lot of words.

I stripped out of my jeans and sweatshirt, and selected a pair of rust-colored slacks and a black silk blouse. The guitar music suddenly stopped. I swear the man has radar. I was stepping into the slacks when Bill appeared in the stateroom doorway. He looked me over and grinned wolfishly.

I had time to shower again and still make it to my lunch date, only now I had a smile on my face.

# CHAPTER 4

I ARRIVED AT MICHELINO'S FIVE MINUTES
early, hoping I'd have a chance to observe
the suspect waitress from a distance before
being seated at a table and becoming distracted
by my conversation with Paul.

The server's name was Martina. She was
in her late-twenties, blonde with brown roots,
slender, very pretty, and tastefully made-up.
She wore the same uniform all the waitstaff
wore at Michelino's: a white shirt, black
slacks, and a white apron. The only noticeable
difference was her shoes, a pair of black
Ferragamo pumps that cost at least six hundred
dollars. Not very practical for someone who
spent eight hours a day on her feet, but they
looked fabulous. Apart from the fact that she
needed her roots touched-up, Martina's hair
was expertly cut and styled. She moved with

grace and confidence and smiled often. I could smell the deceit, even from a distance. I owe this ability to a larcenous period in my own life, of which I am not particularly proud, but for which I am often grateful.

I had a rough childhood, partially because of my cousin Aaron, who convinced my parents that I was responsible for many of his crimes, and partly because my mom is a former nun and my dad was born a Cossack. Aware of the injustice of being punished for offenses that Aaron had committed, I began shoplifting at the age of six. If my parents believed I was bad, I might as well be bad. I graduated to till-tapping excellence during my retail career in my late teens and early twenties. When I accepted a security management position with a chain of department stores, I decided it was time to stop and, over time, I anonymously repaid all that I had stolen. After a few years in management I realized I wasn't happy working for someone else, and decided to put my crime-solving talent to better use. So I gave two months notice, trained my replacement, and went looking for a private investigator who would teach me the craft.

When I met Sam Pettigrew he was sixty. He's just under six feet tall, black, about two hundred and fifty solid pounds, and as cantankerous a human being as I've ever known. Initially I found his lack of manners refreshing because, I thought, if he was allowed to be rude to me, I was allowed to be rude to him. That didn't work out very well.

Paul showed up at Michelino's at 12:59, looked around, and spotted me at the bar. He waved, giving me a strained smile, and I remembered once again how fond I was of him. Time apart doesn't matter when you have a connection with someone.

I asked if he wanted a drink before lunch and he declined, so I flagged down the host and asked for a table, pointing to Martina's section.

Once we were seated she approached promptly, handed us menus, and recited the specials of the day. Ignoring me, she focused her considerable charm on Paul, smiling and occasionally touching his shoulder. I had to admit she was good. What she didn't anticipate was that I would be the one paying the check. It would be fun watching her change gears when she realized the size of her tip would not be influenced by male hormones.

Paul and I made small talk while we looked over our menus. As I observed my old friend I noticed, again, the tension just beneath the surface and the dark circles under his eyes. I hoped he wasn't in financial trouble or suffering from some serious illness.

When Martina returned with my water and Paul's beer, we were ready to order. I asked for the lobster cannelloni. I don't normally eat pasta, but it was the most expensive item on the menu, and if I was going to tempt Martina I had to request a high-ticket entrée. Paul ordered a New York steak with a Caesar salad.

When we were alone again I said, "You're going to have to let me pay for lunch, you know."

"Why would you do that? I asked *you*."

"Because I'm working," I whispered, leaning forward. "I do covert employee surveillance at restaurants and bars. I'll be reimbursed. It's great to see you again, Paul. Now tell me what's wrong. Are you in some kind of trouble? Are you sick?"

"No, nothing like that. It's about my job." He hesitated. "Look, I'm really freaking out over this, Nikki. I desperately need to confide in someone, but you can't tell anybody."

"Okay," I said, feeling a chill. Considering he was an air traffic control supervisor, he now had my full attention.

"Three of the controllers reporting to me have been killed in the last two months," he said, his voice low. "Their deaths were all ruled accidental, but the coincidence is unbelievable."

"You think someone is targeting your co-workers, and making their deaths look like accidents?"

"I do."

"If that's the case, I think we can assume that your life, and those of the other controllers may also be in danger."

"I know." Paul took another sip of his beer and looked at me, a deep furrow between his brows. "What do you think I should do?"

"I think you need someone objective and discreet to look into this. And I think you need to warn your remaining employees, and maybe hire yourself a bodyguard."

"You know how people react to anything that sounds like terrorism these days. For that reason, my bosses have vetoed any additional investigation."

"Let's take this one step at a time. Tell me what you know about the three controllers who were killed." I took out my notepad. "I'll need names, dates, locations, and the circumstances surrounding their deaths. Any details you can give me."

"This could be dangerous. Are you sure you want to get involved?"

"I need more information before I can

answer that question. But yeah, I'd like to help any way I can." I smiled at my old friend and covered his hand with mine.

"Thank you, Nikki. I tried talking to the homicide investigators assigned to the latest death, but they just seem to want the case closed. No evidence of foul play, they said. How can they possibly believe that when three controllers who worked the same shift at the same airport have been killed?"

"Tell me everything," I said.

The first to die had been James Flannery, age forty-seven, father of two, divorced, and living alone. James had died on September 19th when his house blew up at 4:45 a.m., shortly after he arrived home from work. The ATF investigator concluded that there must have been a pinhole rupture in the gas line. Because of the scope of the explosion there was no way to determine what had caused the leak, and there was no sign of arson.

We were interrupted when Martina served Paul's salad. She picked up his napkin and placed it on his lap, making the maneuver look suggestive.

"Enjoy," she purred, before walking away.

I looked forward to busting her if she was till-tapping. She was flirting with my friend just to get a bigger tip, and it was tactless to come on to a male customer who was seated with a female customer. She didn't know we weren't a couple.

Paul took a bite of his salad, and resumed his story. The second controller to die had been a woman named Shirley Jensen. Shirley had been in her thirties, single, and tough. That's the way Paul described her. I imagined someone who took kickboxing classes for fun. Shirley had drowned while scuba diving off the Monterey coast on September 24th. Paul said she had been an expert diver, but there was no evidence recovered that would prove her death had been anything other than accidental. Apparently, her tank had run out of air and she was too deep to make it to the surface. By the time her body was found, both Shirley and her gear were pretty torn up, which impeded the investigation.

I could understand why Paul was suspicious. My friend, Jim Sutherland, enjoys scuba diving and always checks his tank personally before going in the water. He knows exactly how much air he has and how long he can stay down, and he takes no chances. I couldn't imagine an air traffic controller would be any less cautious.

Hearing about a drowning always reminds me of my dad. When I was in my early twenties he went on a solo fishing trip and allegedly drowned, but I never believed it. He was a strong swimmer and an old hand at boating. I'm pretty sure he decided to embark on a new adventure without the emotional entanglements of his family.

Paul had another bite of salad and a sip of his beer. He looked thoughtful. "Of all the people I've worked with since I became a controller," he said, "Shirley is the last one I would have expected to, you know, die. She worked out every day, only ate healthy food, and she wouldn't take crap from anyone." He started to take another swig of beer and seemed surprised to discover his bottle was empty.

I waved at Martina and raised the bottle. She nodded.

"What about the third one?" I asked.

"Gordon Mayes," he said. "A really nice guy. I mean, genuinely nice."

Martina delivered Paul's beer, retrieved the empty, and asked, "How's your salad?"

"It's fine," Paul responded, without looking at her.

She pouted prettily and sauntered away, leaving us alone again.

"How was Gordon killed?" I asked.

Paul looked at me for a moment, his eyes locked on mine. "Thank you," he said, "for asking how he was killed instead of how he died. Gordon was killed in a single car accident. He was driving home from work yesterday morning, a little after four. That was the call I got at the reunion last night. He was on the Highway Ninety-Two overpass near Delaware Street. They think he fell asleep at the wheel and rolled over the retaining wall. Gordon drove an Explorer and he always kept the windows open to help him stay awake. I talked to the detectives this morning, and they said the only unusual thing they found in his car was a charred rubber snake. They asked me if he had any kids. He didn't."

*Rubber snake?*

"I know that overpass," I said. What I didn't say was that I knew it was treacherous. I didn't want to imply that it might have been an accident. "You've obviously been thinking a lot about this. Do you have any theories?"

"Not really. I suppose it could be some kind of terrorist organization, but there's one thing I'm certain of. These deaths are connected and none of them were accidental. I feel it in my bones, Nikki."

Martina approached and served our entrées. I was grateful for the interruption because I needed a moment to think. I'd worked a couple of homicide cases, but I had no experience with multi-jurisdictional crimes of this nature. I wasn't even sure where to begin. Plus, being as fond as I am of Paul might be a disadvantage. I'd be worried about him and that would distract me. On the other hand, because I cared about him, I would probably be more aware of the danger to him than some stranger he might turn to.

We ate our lunch in silence, both of us lost in thought, although regardless of my concern about Paul's situation, it was impossible to ignore the creamy texture and rich garlic and basil piquancy of my lobster cannelloni. Every bite melted in my mouth. It was a delicious distraction from the horrific story Paul had shared with me.

When Martina collected the plates and offered coffee and desert, I asked for the check. She froze for an instant, then graced me with her magnetic smile. I smiled back.

She returned three minutes later with a black leather folder containing a hand-written list of the food and beverages we had ordered. The prices were correct and so was the total, but I had seen this ploy before. Rather than paying with a credit card, I gave Martina a little more rope and paid with cash, sliding four twenties into the folder and handing it back to her.

I kept an eye on her as she went behind the

bar where the food servers record their orders. There are only two registers at Michelino's, and both are behind the bar. I was able to see the register Martina used from where we were sitting, but just barely. It looked to me like the display showed 0.00, which would indicate a no-sale. I noted the time. It would be easy enough to check later. Besides, if she had recorded the sale properly she would bring me a cash register receipt.

After stopping at a couple of other tables, Martina returned the leather folder to me, said, "Thank you," and sashayed off. I opened the folder and discovered my change and a carbon copy of the hand written, itemized tab. Very inventive. Only someone who knew the routine at Michelino's would know something was amiss. I left a miserly fifteen percent gratuity and pocketed the hand-written receipt.

As we were walking out of the restaurant I said, "I'll need to involve someone else in this case, Paul. It sounds urgent to me."

"Is it someone you trust?" Paul asked. "I can't risk having anything leak to the press."

"I trust him with my life and, believe me, he won't talk to the press or to anyone else about the investigation."

"Okay. Who is it?"

"The PI who trained me," I said. "Sam Pettigrew."

# CHAPTER 5

SAMSON PETTIGREW IS A GRIZZLED old coot, but he was the best teacher I could have hoped for. He taught me to question everything, never take anything for granted, and never assume that appearances translate to reality. We'd had some pretty heated arguments about this during my internship because of my tendency to be literal.

I adore Sam, but he's a pain in the ass, so most of the time I love him from a distance. It's easier that way. In the two-plus years since I earned my PI license I've called Sam only a handful of times, to ask him questions I couldn't find the answers to online, but I've never called because I really needed help. If Paul was right, and the three recent deaths were not accidental, then he was almost certainly on the killer's short list. If I didn't act fast enough he could lose his life. Because I wasn't willing to take that chance, and because Sam has more than thirty years of experience, I needed him now.

These thoughts were swirling around in my head as I drove to Sunnyvale on Saturday afternoon. I knew Sam would be working. Sam always works on Saturdays. He claims it's the only time he can get his reports written, because he can lock the door and ignore the phone.

I parked behind the Round Table Pizza a couple of doors down from Pettigrew Investigations, locked my car, and took a deep breath before approaching my old training ground. I still had a key to the office. Sam hadn't asked me to return it when I left, and I hadn't volunteered to part with it.

I knocked briskly on the outer office door and peered through the glass down the hall to where I knew Sam was contemplating whether or not to respond. I gave him a full minute before knocking a second time. This time I followed the knock with a shout. "Hey, Sam, it's *Nikki!*"

Another ten seconds passed while I pictured him hauling himself up from his leather swivel chair, squeezing between his desk and the wall, and walking to the door of his private office. I'd gotten really pissed off at Sam one day when I was working for him, and had moved his desk an inch closer to the wall while he was in the bathroom. You should have heard the language.

Suddenly there he was, peering down the hallway to the glass-paned door where I stood gazing back at him. I waved. He stood, staring at me for a moment. I almost missed the smile, it was on his lips so briefly. Then he ambled slowly toward me.

Sam Pettigrew is a big man and his dusky brown complexion is accented by a pair of keen dark eyes that could snap your neck from thirty paces.

"Well I'll be damned," he said, from the other side of the door. "I was beginning to wonder if I'd ever see you again." He squinted at me through his bifocals. "What the hell happened to your face, girl?"

I've become so accustomed to the specks of embedded gunpowder in my temple that I hardly notice them anymore, unless someone points them out. My hand automatically went to my face and I flushed at the memory.

"There was this psycho killer. You probably read about it in the paper," I said. "Open the damn door!"

Sam let me in and looked me up and down

like a parent examining a wayward child. I fought the urge to hug him and lost. I threw my arms around his burly shoulders and he squirmed with discomfort. When I released him he turned away from me to lock the door. I thought I saw him dash at his eyes under his glasses, but I might have imagined it.

The office smelled of cigar smoke and coffee, like it always had.

Sam turned back toward his inner sanctum and shouted over his shoulder, "What do you need, Nicoli? Must be important, to get you all the way down here to Sunnyvale. What is it, fifteen miles from home for you?"

I felt the sting, as he had intended me to. At the same time I couldn't help feeling amused at the strange way Sam has of expressing affection.

"I missed you too, you old goat. I'm sorry I haven't come for a visit. And yes, I need your help on a case, and it's important."

Over coffee, I explained the situation with Paul and his coworkers. Sam listened silently until I was finished, then he took off his glasses and wiped them with a handkerchief.

"The first question you need to ask in a situation like this," he said, "is what's the motive. You find the motive, you can find the person behind these killings. You need to look into any accidents in the last year or so that took place while the dead controllers were on duty. You said they all worked the same shift, right?"

"Yes." I started taking notes.

"That's a break. If it was random, or just some nut with a grudge against air traffic controllers, or even someone who wanted to increase the likelihood of air traffic disasters, they wouldn't care what shift these people worked. If all the victims worked the same shift, odds are something happened during that shift. You find out what that was, you can generate a list of suspects."

"You don't think we should look at disgruntled employees?" I asked.

"Disgruntled employees usually kill their boss first."

"Sam, will you work with me on this case?" I winced at the feeling of vulnerability, and held my breath waiting for his response.

He rubbed the bridge of his nose for a moment, then put his glasses back on. "I might have some time to help you," he said. "But you'd have to handle a couple of jobs for me while I'm doing it. Can't neglect my regular clients."

"Sure, but we need to get started immediately, and we need to keep a low profile. Paul made it clear he can't afford to have anything leak to the press. I'm amazed it hasn't already."

"That's because there's no evidence these deaths were homicides. Once we start digging around and uncover that evidence, all hell's gonna break loose. There are leaks in every police department. Cops don't make enough money to refuse bribes from the press. Can your friend get you a list of all the accidents that have taken place during his shift in the last year?"

"I'll ask." I made a note. "What else?"

"You just get me the list of accidents, and a list of all the passengers and employees who were injured or killed in those accidents. And then we'll get started. We should also have the names and addresses of the other controllers on the shift, the ones who are still alive, because they're potential victims."

"Thank you, Sam."

"Don't thank me yet," he said, looking me square in the eye.

I understood the implication. Even if we did find out who the killer was, it might be too late. Someone else might die. Paul might die. I really didn't want to think about that.

On my way back to Redwood City, I called Paul on my cell and asked him for the accident reports for the last year, and the passenger and employee lists.

He was silent for a long moment. Then he said, "You don't need a year's worth of records. You only need six months. Gordon was new on the graveyard shift. He just started in April."

"Great. That will save time. When can you get me the records?"

"I'll print them out for you tomorrow night, when I'm back at work."

"Thanks, and Paul, I'd like you to think about hiring a bodyguard."

"How much would something like that cost?" he asked.

"I know a local cop who charges sixty an hour plus mileage. It sounds like a lot, until you consider the alternative."

I still had Quinn's contact info in my smartphone. I pulled over long enough to give her name and phone number to Paul. Bill had recommended Lieutenant Quinn to me a few months ago, when I was in need of protection. I'd never actually used her services, but I'd called her for a rate quote and had liked her instantly.

"Maybe I'll give her a call," he said. "What's your fax number so I can send the information to you?"

"It's on the business card I gave you last night."

"Okay. Make sure your paper tray is full."

# CHAPTER 6

WHEN I GOT BACK TO the office I loaded the fax paper tray first thing. Then I typed up my report on the waitress, Martina. When I was satisfied that I'd covered every possible detail of the lunch surveillance, I printed the report and an invoice and photocopied the hand-written receipt Martina had substituted for a cash register receipt. I stuffed the whole thing in a FedEx envelope and walked to the drop box outside the marina management office. Some of my clients prefer having their reports e-mailed to them, but Michelino's owner was old school, and only wanted hard copies.

Between the office buildings and the water are cobblestone walkways, a wide expanse of lawn, and an assortment of trees and well maintained flowering plants. I think of the docks and the yachts as the heart of the marina complex.

Back in my office I gazed out at the scenery. Two of my office walls are almost floor-to-ceiling windows that slide open, so from my desk I can see most of the marina: everything from the lawn to the inlet off the bay, my boat and my neighbors' boats, weeping willow trees and azalea bushes, and the odd cluster of cattails. The view almost never fails to relax me, but today it did nothing to ease the knot of tension in my gut.

I spent half an hour going over my schedule for the week, looking to see what I could postpone until after Paul's case was somehow resolved. I could do four bar and restaurant surveys a night if I started early and stayed out late. That would free up my days for Paul. I made a list of the places I thought had the greatest likelihood of employee theft, and threw in a couple that weren't high risk but that I didn't want to neglect, out of respect for the owners. I tucked the list in my purse, locked up the office, and walked down to my boat.

It was four o'clock. I'd hardly slept the night before and I needed a power nap if I was going to work late. The boat was silent as I stepped aboard, but that didn't mean it was vacant. Bill was probably either reading or online. When he's not working a case, he spends the occasional weekend onboard with me. He owns a two-bedroom house on Madison Avenue in Redwood City, but I think being on the water feels like a vacation to him.

"Hello?" I called out, as I climbed down the steps into the galley.

"In here," he answered from the main salon.

On my way through the galley I opened the refrigerator and grabbed a Guinness Stout and a bottle opener. I gave Bill a kiss, opened the bottle, and looked over his shoulder at the computer. He takes his laptop everywhere with him. He was in a firearms chat room with a bunch of other law enforcement officers, or LEOs, discussing second amendment rights and gun control. He finished typing a response and sent it, then turned to look me over. He took the open bottle out of my hand.

"You need a nap," he said, taking a sip.

"I know. Couldn't sleep last night. Join me?"

Bill set the Stout bottle on top of the built-in bureau, took me by the hand, and led me back to the stateroom.

"If I join you, you won't get any sleep," he murmured.

"Sleep is highly overrated."

He sat me down on the bunk, took off my shoes, and pushed me back onto the pillows. He pulled the comforter over me, kissed me on the forehead, and left the room. I closed my eyes for a moment, and the next thing I knew it was dark outside.

"*Shit,*" I said, struggling into a sitting position. "God damn it, I have to work tonight! Why'd you let me sleep so long?"

"Relax," came Bill's unconcerned response from the direction of the galley. "You were tired, and it's only six-thirty. I'll make coffee."

Bill is often the voice of sanity in my otherwise hectic life. While I'm rushing around having anxiety attacks, he's moving steadily toward the resolution of whatever situation he's in. I wish I could relax in the face of the unknown. Hell, I wish I could relax period. Ever since I quit smoking I've been crawling with nervous energy. Before I quit, whenever I felt like my head was going to explode, I'd just have a cigarette and that would take the tension down a notch. Now I have to deal with what I'm feeling. I don't mind the good feelings, but anxiety sucks.

I groped for the bedside lamp and took a couple of slow deep breaths. Bill appeared in the doorway.

"Sorry I snapped," I said. "I have to get

as many surveys out of the way as possible before things start moving on this air traffic controller thing."

"I forgive you. What air traffic controller thing?"

"My friend Paul, the one you met at the reunion, is an ATC supervisor. Three graveyard shift controllers reporting to him have died mysteriously in the last two months and Paul doesn't believe their deaths were accidental. I'm looking into it."

"Is this the same Paul that was kneeling at your feet and begged you to have lunch with him?"

"Yep. Jealous?"

"You wish. Why didn't you say anything last night?"

"I didn't find out about it until lunch today, and I shouldn't even be telling you now. Paul swore me to secrecy, so you can't mention this investigation to anyone. His bosses are totally paranoid about the press catching wind of it."

"Not a problem."

"Anyway, I have to do a few surveys tonight. You want to come out with me? I could use a beard."

A beard is what we PIs call someone who accompanies us on a surveillance so we don't look out of place. A couple makes more sense when you're doing restaurant and bar surveys. People eating or drinking alone tend to stand out.

"I could eat," he said. "Where are we going?"

I dug in my purse and handed him the list.

"Wow," he said. "Good thing I skipped lunch."

I drank two cups of coffee and started perking up. I dressed in black slacks and a turquoise cashmere sweater, scrunched my curls into submission, touched up my mascara, and slathered on some plum-colored lip-gloss.

"Ready to go?" Bill asked.

I looked up from the mirror and took in the vision before me. Wearing a white shirt open at the neck, a pair of black jeans that hugged his butt, and a luminous smile, Bill Anderson was a beautiful man. Not a pretty boy, but ruggedly-handsome-with-a-twinkle-in-his-hazel-eyes-take-your-breath-away beautiful. Of course knowing how he feels about me adds something to what I see when I look at him.

"You're going to distract me," I said.

# CHAPTER 7

WE STARTED THE EVENING AT Chez
Jacques, which is located on the
southern-most tip of Redwood City, where
it borders Atherton. One of the few French
restaurants on the Peninsula, Chez Jacques
rates a full five stars in the Silicon Valley
Restaurant Guide. Luckily the portions are
typically French, which means tiny. We
ordered entrées, but no appetizers, no salad,
and no wine. When you're going to have three
dinners in one night you need to eat light and
stay sober.

Our waiter, Francois, sounded
authentically French and looked disdainfully
down his aquiline nose as he took our orders.
That would go in my report. Many French
restaurants encourage their serving staff to
be aloof with patrons, but Chez Jacques is

not among them. The owner, Jessica James, maintains a very high standard of customer service. Jessica and I got to know each other when I was working department store security. She managed the restaurant in the Millbrae store. Now she owns Chez Jacques in Atherton and the Garden Grill in Menlo Park. I've been doing one survey a week at each of her restaurants since I got my license. The food is so good I almost feel guilty charging for my services.

Francois was new. I hadn't seen him before at either of Jessica's restaurants. I was surprised she had hired a new food server without having me do a pre-employment background check. He might be a relative of one of the cooks or one of the other food servers. Maybe he was temporarily filling in for someone who was out sick.

The conversation among the diners was subdued, as was the lighting, but the scents wafting from passing trays were not and made my mouth water.

I kept an eye on Francois as he served other tables and attempted to make eye contact when he delivered our entrées. He never met my gaze. He set the plates on the table, serving first me and then Bill, nodded curtly, and muttered, "Bon appétit," before sauntering away.

The food was exquisite, as always. The cuisine is never an issue at Jessica's restaurants. I had ordered the Loup de Mer, a lightly grilled Mediterranean seabass filet, which was nestled atop a pool of buttery lemon sauce, crème fraiche, and steamed spinach, and crowned with a single sprig of rosemary. It was a struggle for me not to lick the plate clean, but I managed.

After Chez Jacques, Bill and I drove north to Burlingame. On the way, I told him about my visit with Sam Pettigrew. He raised an eyebrow when I told him I'd asked Sam for help, but didn't comment.

We covered two more restaurants and two bars that night. The last stop was in San Francisco. When we were driving back to Redwood City on Highway 101, I glanced over at SFO and wondered where the air traffic control tower was. Was it really a tower? All that was required was a room full of radar equipment and a group of highly skilled, very intelligent, and calm-in-a-crisis people, right?

We arrived back at the marina at 1:23 a.m., gathered up our leftovers, and walked down to the docks. It was low tide and the companionway was steep. I filled my lungs with the pungent fragrance of seaweed. Unlike some boat dwellers, I love the marina smells.

We stopped at Kirk's Bluewater 42, because D'Artagnon was sprawled on the bow, and offered him a sampling of what we had in our doggie bags. D'Artagnon is always hungry, but tonight he seemed unenthusiastic about the table scraps. In fact, he remained lying down on the deck.

I reached out to pet him while Bill fed him a few bites of steak. "What's wrong, boy? I asked, stroking his ears. "I hope he's okay," I said to Bill. "I've noticed his limp is getting worse. I think I'll drop in on Kirk tomorrow."

I felt a tightness in my chest as we walked the remaining distance to my boat.

# CHAPTER 8

SUNDAY MORNING I LET BILL sleep in while I filled my thermal mug with coffee and walked down the dock to Kirk's yacht. I knocked on the starboard window and waited. Kirk is a marketing analyst and a sensitive, if slightly macho, guy. His son, Jonathan, lived with him until he went away to college, but he comes home during the summer months. Kirk's father also makes frequent visits to the marina, but I've never seen Kirk in the company of a woman. My impression is that his divorce from Jonathan's mom left him emotionally scarred.

I could smell bacon cooking, so I knew he was home. D'Artagnon was nowhere in sight, but it was early yet. After a moment the blinds went up and Kirk slid the window open. He was smiling, but the smile didn't reach his eyes.

"Is D'Artagnon okay?" I asked. "I've noticed the limp is getting worse and when we stopped to feed him treats last night he didn't seem to have much of an appetite."

"It's his arthritis. The vet gave me some steroidal anti-inflammatories to feed him, but they ruin his appetite. I'm worried about his quality of life. Eating's the most important thing in the world to D'Artagnon. I hate spoiling that for him."

"What does the vet say about taking him for walks?"

"He's having trouble getting on and off the boat, but he still loves going for walks. The vet said walking is good for him, but to take it slow. I've gotta go," he said, blinking away tears. "Bacon's burning." He closed the window and lowered the blinds.

I put on my sunglasses and walked back to my boat. Bill was in the galley drinking coffee when I came down the companionway. I told him what Kirk had said. I'm overly sentimental about dogs and D'Artagnon is my favorite canine. I knew what Kirk was going through.

I planned a trip to the gym, followed by a couple of lunch surveys and, later, a dinner survey and three bars. Maybe if I was focused on employee performance I wouldn't worry so much about D'Artagnon.

I put on shorts and a tee shirt, and drove around the corner to the Athletic Center. I jogged on the treadmill, climbed on the Stairmaster, and hoisted free weights until my arms trembled. Then I did a hundred crunches and fifty military pushups. I showered and changed at the gym before going to work.

I spent the afternoon and early evening driving, eating, drinking, and scribbling notes about how well other people were doing their jobs. No one appeared to be stealing from my clients, so the reports would focus on the quality of service and cuisine, the ambiance and cleanliness of the restaurants and bars, and the disposition of the patrons.

I checked my office fax machine when I got back, but Paul hadn't sent the accident reports yet. I walked down to the boat, stopping to pet D'Artagnon along the way. He seemed a little more energetic than he had the night before. I knocked on Kirk's window and asked if he could help D'Artagnon off the boat so I could to take him for a walk. Then I went home to change clothes again, and found Bill in the main salon playing his guitar.

"I'm taking D'Artagnon to the wildlife refuge for a walk," I said, as I pulled on an old pair of jeans and my Ecco Track II boots.

"Want some company?"

I thought about it for a minute and decided that I wanted to be alone with D'Artagnon. "Not this time," I said. "But thanks for asking."

I grabbed a bottle of water in case one of us got thirsty, stuffed some small dog biscuits into my pockets, and hustled back to Kirk's boat. D'Artagnon was standing on the bow wagging his tail, as though he was expecting me.

"Did you want to go for a walk?" I asked.

The wagging increased in velocity until his tail was spinning like a propeller.

Kirk was waiting for him on the swim platform. D'Artagnon padded to the stern of the boat, and Kirk lifted him, setting him gently on the dock. I snagged the leash Kirk keeps on a hook and attached it to his collar. The pup moved slowly, but his tail kept spinning so I figured he was okay.

We walked across the street to the Bair Island wildlife refuge. This was D'Artagnon's favorite place because there were so many wonderful smells: other dogs, rabbits, rats, squirrels, herons, and who knows what else. There's a three-mile path that winds around the refuge. It gets muddy in the fall and winter, but wasn't too bad tonight.

As we walked, D'Artagnon sniffed the air, the ground, and the bushes. I stroked his back whenever he stopped walking, and fed him the dog biscuits one at a time.

After half an hour he started to tire, panting and moving more slowly. I knelt down and poured some water from the bottle into my hand, and he drank. Then he licked my face and allowed me to hug him, wagging serenely.

When we got back to the marina I rinsed his feet and my boots with the hose, and returned him to Kirk. I received another lick on the nose from the grateful pup, and retreated to my office.

The fax tray was still empty, so I occupied myself typing up the surveys I'd conducted earlier in the day. I called down to the boat to let Bill know where I was. I felt guilty that I'd been neglecting him in favor of work and D'artagnon, and the weekend was almost over. While we were on the phone my fax started ringing.

# CHAPTER 9

TWO HUNDRED AND TWENTY-TWO PAGES rolled out of my fax machine that night. I had to reload the paper tray twice.

Bill joined me in the office and we scanned the reports as they came in. There were four airline accident reports, but only one with fatalities. Each began with an identification number and the date on which the accident had occurred. They included flight numbers, a chronological history of each flight, the type of aircraft involved, location of the accident, aids to navigation, and meteorological data collected from the national weather service. There were also lists of injured persons and, in the one case, fatalities.

I didn't understand a lot of what I was reading, but I felt certain the answer lay in the fatalities, so that's what I focused on. I copied the whole thing, flagging the pages with lists of names on them. I would take the original to Sam in the morning.

Bill hadn't had dinner, so at 10:30 he went out. Forty minutes later he was back with an extra large pizza. He ate, and I drank coffee, and we both read the pages about the accident that had included fatalities. I opened a blank Excel spreadsheet, and as Bill read me the names of the deceased passengers and employees I entered the data.

Around midnight my vision started blurring. We left everything on my desk except the leftover pizza, which we broke into bite-sized pieces and delivered to the bow of Kirk's boat. The scent would probably wake D'Artagnon and he'd have a nice surprise.

$$\sim \cdots \sim$$

First thing Monday morning I called Sam. He's not a morning person, but he is a creature of habit and always arrives at the office early.

"Pettigrew Investigations," he grumbled.

"Good morning. I've got those accident reports for you."

"Finally! Bring 'em on down."

"Is now a good time?" I asked.

"No, but it can't wait. You'll have to do a couple surveys for me today so I'll have time to look 'em over. Hit the road, Nicoli. There's work to be done." And he hung up.

I looked at my watch. It was 8:02. Sam always did donut shop surveys on Monday mornings. Oh my *God*, he was going to ask me to survey the House of Donuts. I hated doing the donut shops. My will power weakens around just about anything covered with chocolate.

I arrived at Sam's office in less than twenty minutes, handed him the two hundred and twenty-two pages plus a copy of my Excel spreadsheet, and poured myself a cup of coffee.

"Don't get comfortable," he said. "I need you to go right back out."

"Not the House of Donuts," I whined.

"Hey, they pay on time. What, are you too good to survey donut shops now that you're investigating murders all the damn time?"

"I do bar and restaurant surveys every week, Sam. It's just the frickin' *chocolate*."

"So don't buy the chocolate. Suck it up, Nicoli. I need you to do the Sunnyvale, Mountain View, and Redwood City stores before ten."

"Why didn't you tell me that before I drove all the way down here from Redwood City?"

"Because I wanted to get my hands on these reports so I can help you save your friend's life. Or have you forgotten I'm doing you a favor?"

I flinched at the rebuke. "Sorry. I'll go quietly."

Leaving Sam with the accident reports I drove from Sunnyvale to Redwood City and back, purchasing chocolate and glazed donuts, bagels and cream cheese, large cups of coffee, and House of Donuts designer mugs, all with cash.

When the cashier in the Redwood City store failed to record my sale on the register, I thought I might have caught myself a till-tapper, but she politely explained that the register was broken and asked if I wanted her to hand-write a receipt for me. I said yes, since I was buying for everyone at the office and needed them to pay me back. She itemized the hand-written receipt, and by the time she'd finished there were five people waiting in line behind me. I felt bad about that until the following week, when Sam told me he'd submitted my report to the owner, who said the register in the Redwood City store was new and had never malfunctioned.

When I arrived back at Sam's office he was surrounded by the accident report pages. I started to say something, but he held up his hand to stop me, so I clamped my mouth shut, remembering that I owed him big for helping me with the investigation.

I went to the desk in the outer office where I had sat for the two years I'd worked for Sam whenever I had surveillance reports to compose, and typed up the three donut shop surveys on his old Macintosh computer. As I was printing the reports, Sam came out of his office and said, "Did you bring me anything?"

I pointed to the coffee table where I'd left all the donuts, bagels, coffee, and mugs I had purchased. I hadn't eaten a thing and was extremely proud of myself.

"So what do you think?" I asked, eager to hear what he had to say.

Sam selected one of the chocolate glazed donuts, which is among my favorite poisons, and took a huge bite. My mouth started watering and I fished in my purse for a pack of the sugarless gum I started chewing when I quit smoking. I found the pack and stuffed two pieces into my mouth. He took another bite of his donut, opened one of the coffees, and motioned me back to his office. I grabbed a coffee and followed.

I sat across from him and looked at the piles of fax paper spread across his desk. I started to comment on the mess, and then remembered that my desk was no better. I closed my mouth before the words could escape.

Sam swallowed the last bite of donut, licked his fingers, took a sip of coffee, and pointed to the stack on his left. Beneath his finger was the spreadsheet I had created. I looked closer and noticed that Sam had highlighted several of the names.

"One of these people is most likely related to your killer. In each case two or more family members were killed and the cause of this accident was never determined, at least not yet. If you were a person prone to placing blame, and you lost your whole family in a plane crash, and then the airline told you they didn't know why the plane had crashed, you might go a little bit postal."

Sam sipped more coffee and I picked up the spreadsheet and looked more closely at the names he had highlighted. "Okay," I said. "So we need to research the surviving members of each of these families."

"We can't do actual background checks without some information to start with, but your friend can probably get you the next of kin information. They'd need that for the notification process. Then we can casually drop in on them, maybe pretend we're with the

NATCA investigative committee or something like that, and scope 'em out."

"NATCA?"

"National Air Traffic Controllers Association."

"I'll call Paul. Thank you, Sam."

"Don't thank me yet," he repeated.

"Oh for Christ's sake," I said. "I'll call you when I have more information."

"Don't go off on your own with this, Nicoli. I don't want you knocking on the killer's door without backup."

"I won't. I promise."

I drove back to Redwood City thinking about my relationship with Sam and wondering if I'd assigned him the role of substitute father. My dad had also been gruff, and hadn't expressed affection easily. I knew Sam cared about me, but I'd never stopped by just to visit. Maybe I was subconsciously punishing my father for his disappearance from my life by staying away from Sam. Sometimes I'm too complex for my own good.

I called Paul at home while I was driving back to Redwood City. It was 11:15, and his shift didn't start until 7:00 p.m. He was probably still asleep. His voicemail picked up and I pulled to the side of the road so I could read the list. I left a message, including the names Sam had highlighted, saying I needed information on their next of kin as soon as possible. When I disconnected I felt a wave of fear slide through my stomach. What if Paul hadn't answered because the killer had already struck again? Or what if he was home but he had company? Maybe I shouldn't have left such explicit information on his machine. *Crap!*

I arrived at the marina thinking I wanted a snack. Lately, when I crave nicotine and gum isn't doing the trick, I've been using food as an antidote for anxiety. I stopped to see if Kirk was home, but he didn't respond to my knock, and D'Artagnon wasn't out on deck.

I walked down the dock, and as I approached Frank and Rocky's boat—that would be Frank the human and Rocky the Chow mix—I spotted a big red-haired puppy tied to Frank's dock box. I knew he was a puppy because his feet were too big for the rest of him. He was wagging his tail and whining softly at the same time. Naturally I stopped to say hello. I hadn't met this dog before, but Frank often rescues strays. I squatted down and he licked my face.

"Hey, Frank!" I shouted. "Who's *this*?"

Frank popped his head out of the hatch, and said, "That's Buddy. He followed Rocky home like they were friends, so I named him

Buddy. No collar. Probably abandoned. He was hungry. I can't bring him aboard because he isn't neutered and neither is Rocky. Whenever I let him on the boat Rocky tries to mount him. I'm afraid they'll get into a fight."

While we were talking, Rocky was leaning as far as he could over the net that kept him on the deck of Frank's sailboat, trying to get closer to the other dog.

"What are you going to do with him?" I asked.

"I thought I'd put up pictures of him around the neighborhood and see if anyone claims him. If they don't, I'll have to take him to the pound."

"Oh *no*. He's so sweet. I'm sure his people must be worried sick."

I scratched Buddy's ears some more, told him everything would be okay, and then walked the remaining distance to my boat. I could feel the puppy's eyes on my back all the way down the dock. I turned and looked back as I stepped aboard, and sure enough, he was looking right at me. Making eye contact is intimidating for most dogs, but not this guy, and he had that sad hound look nailed. If I wasn't careful, I was going to end up with a roommate.

I had cottage cheese and rice cakes for

DINNER AND A MURDER

lunch, but I didn't feel any better, so I tried calling Paul again. This time he answered on the second ring and relief washed over me.

"I got your message," he said. "Sorry I missed your call. I was outside working in the garden."

"You shouldn't expose yourself like that. What if you're next on the killer's list?"

There was silence on the other end of the line for a moment, and then Paul said, "I think I can get you the next of kin information tonight. It might take a little digging, but I should be able to fax it to you by morning."

"Thanks. You have to be more careful, Paul. Try to think defensively. Have you called Quinn yet?"

"No."

"You need to do that."

As soon as we hung up my phone rang. It was Steve Saxon.

"You're not serious about that cop you brought to the reunion, are you?" he said without preamble. "Come to Maine. I'll fly you out first class."

"How did you get my number?" I asked, offended by how easily he had dismissed Bill.

"Bella gave it to me."

I'd have to speak with Bella about giving out personal information without asking first.

"I'm flattered, Steve, but I *am* serious about Bill and, even if I wasn't, I'm not into casual sex."

"Really," he said, a hint of smug self-satisfaction in his voice. "I remember you being a lot more relaxed in high school."

"Will you do me a favor?" I asked, sweetly. "Will you take my phone number and shove it up your ass?" And I hung up.

Now I really needed to talk to Elizabeth. I hadn't seen her since before the reunion. I dialed her work number and she picked up on the first ring.

"Where have you been?" I asked.

"Hi, honey. I spent the weekend with Jack. I guess I should have called you so you wouldn't worry."

"Are you moving in?" I asked, holding my breath.

"Of course not. It's just such a nice house and I'm totally in love with him, but I'm not sure he's ready for a commitment."

"Why do you think that?"

"Because if Jack McGuire was ready for a commitment I'd have a rock the size of a bowling ball on my left hand."

"Maybe he hasn't found a ring he likes. Has he asked you to move in?"

"A couple of times, but I don't want to

move in with him unless he intends to marry me. Is that ridiculous?"

"I think it's intelligent, if marriage is what you really want."

"Have you and Bill talked about marriage?"

"You know I suck at being married."

"People change, Nikki. I'll be home tonight if you want to get together. I'll cook you dinner."

"That sounds great. I need to talk to you about an investigation I'm working on."

"Is it dangerous?"

Elizabeth loves danger, which accounts at least in part for her attraction to a retired cat burglar.

"Very dangerous. Multiple homicides."

"Oh my *God!* What do you want for dinner?"

"Chocolate."

"I'll see you at six," Elizabeth laughed. "Bring wine."

On my way to the parking lot I stopped again to commune with the red-haired pup. I had a few dog biscuits in my pocket, so I squatted down and fed them to him. He licked my face between bites and when he'd finished the last biscuit he turned around and planted his big puppy butt in my lap, forcing me into a sitting position. When he had me where he wanted me, he scooted onto my belly, pushing me flat on my back. He felt like he weighed at least sixty pounds. His tail was wagging and whipping me in the face. I lay there for a minute, enjoying the absurdity of the situation, before pushing him off. He turned around and licked my face again as I got to my feet. This dog belonged on somebody's sofa.

I cruised down El Camino to Beltramo's Wines And Spirits in Atherton so I could buy something nice for my dinner with Elizabeth. One of Beltramo's sommeliers assisted me in selecting a French wine called a Beaune Premier Cru. He told me it had an open and pleasant nose reminiscent of red current, humus, and undergrowth, which would evolve as the wine was allowed to breathe towards touches of spice and vanilla. Sounded good to me. The price was a bit steep, but I really wanted to show Elizabeth how much I appreciate her friendship.

I drove back to the office, deposited the Beltramo's bag on my desk, and opened the Excel workbook where I log my survey schedule. I selected two restaurants, one of which was a new client, and a bar that had an employee I needed to check out, and went to work.

After nibbling on a crab salad at a seafood

joint in Palo Alto, and sipping a Campari and soda at a trendy bistro in Los Altos, I went to a country-western steakhouse in Mountain View. There were peanut shells on the floor, and three couples were waiting to be seated when I arrived. I scoped out the staff and diners while I was waiting to be seated. The country music was so loud it was almost impossible to hear what anyone was saying, but the customers all appeared to be enjoying themselves.

After about fifteen minutes the host seated me in a booth near the jukebox and I was approached by a Latino Adonis in his mid-twenties. His name tag read Juan. He was dressed in tight-fitting jeans and a navy tee shirt, with a white apron tied around his waist. He placed a small bowl of peanuts on the table, handed me a laminated menu, and asked if I'd like something to drink. I requested a Sapphire martini with four olives, and told him to have the bartender put the vermouth in the glass, meaning I wanted to actually taste it.

While I waited for my drink, I perused the menu. This was the first time I'd surveyed this steakhouse, so I read each item on the menu before deciding on the braised shrimp with wild rice and a side salad.

Juan returned with my cocktail and took

my order. When he'd moved on to another table I took a sip of the martini. Being a connoisseur of fine gin, I was able to determine that the bartender had used regular Bombay, and not the Bombay Sapphire I'd requested. Also, there were only three olives in the glass, and I'd requested four. I'd mention these details in my report, but I'd have to check out the bartender before leaving to see if he was neglectful, distracted by the crowd, or simply didn't have Sapphire behind the bar, and was running low on olives.

Juan was charming, but extremely busy with all of his tables. When he served my entrée he removed a bundle of silverware wrapped in a single ply napkin from his apron pocket and placed it on the table next to my plate, but neglected to serve me ice water. He'd also forgotten to bring me the salad I'd ordered. I didn't say anything about the missing salad, and a few minutes later he delivered it, along with an apology, but still no ice water.

By 5:00 I had a mild buzz from the few sips of martini I'd allowed myself. I'd eaten a little of the salad and a few of the braised shrimp. The food was good, if a bit salty for my taste, but I was saving my appetite for dinner with Elizabeth. I waved Juan over to the table and asked for the check. He withdrew two black leather folders from his apron pocket, checked to see which one was mine, and placed it on the table. A cash register receipt showed the items I'd ordered with the correct prices. I took out enough cash to cover the tab and Juan's tip, placed the cash in the folder, and withdrew the receipt.

On my way out of the restaurant I made a brief stop in the bar. The bartender was Hispanic, in his late-thirties, and dressed as Juan had been. He looked harried as he tried to keep up with the number of customers and waitstaff who were anxious for their orders. This was another detail my new client would hear about from me. This poor guy shouldn't have been the only bartender on duty.

They did not, in fact, have Bombay Sapphire available, and I made a mental note to suggest to the owner that it wouldn't hurt to stock a bottle or two for their more discriminating clientele. Even though the restaurant was on the rustic side, they had a full bar, which should be well stocked. The condiment dispenser was filled with olives, so the missing one from my drink was an oversight, either by the bartender or by Juan. I suspected that a few additional staff members would take care of most of my new client's problems.

When I arrived back at the marina I dropped off my survey notes at the office before grabbing the bottle of wine I'd purchased at Beltramo's and walking down to the dock. It wasn't yet time for my dinner with Elizabeth, and I needed to freshen up first anyway, so I headed for my boat. Once again D'Artagnon wasn't on the bow of Kirk's boat, and my heart did a painful clutch in my chest as I wondered why.

When I passed Frank's boat I immediately noticed that the red-haired dog was gone and Rocky, Frank's Chow mix, was moping on deck. Maybe Frank had already found Buddy's family. For some reason the thought made me sad.

I showered onboard and dressed in jeans and a festive Hawaiian shirt. I stuffed a few dog biscuits into the pockets of my jacket, picked up the Beaune Cru, and walked back to Frank's boat. I knocked on the hull and was feeding Rocky a biscuit when Frank came out on deck.

"Where's Buddy?" I asked.

"The Humane Society came and got him," he said.

"Oh, *no*," I said. "I thought you were looking for his family!" I was unable to keep the accusation out of my voice.

"I couldn't just leave him tied to the dock box twenty-four hours a day. You want him? *You* go get him out of jail. I have to go to work." And with that he dropped back inside his boat.

Obviously Frank was feeling some guilt about turning Buddy over to the authorities. Frank always gets pissy when he feels guilty about something. We've been neighbors for a while now, and I've observed this behavior on more than one occasion.

There was a knot in my stomach as I approached D'Artagnon's boat. He still wasn't outside, and when I knocked on Kirk's galley window there was no answer. I left my offering of dog biscuits on the bow, hoping they'd be gone by the time I passed by again.

# CHAPTER 10

I WALKED ON DOWN THE DOCK to Elizabeth's trawler and rapped on the deck outside her open door.

"Come on in, honey," she called out.

I boarded the boat and gave her a hug, inhaling the aroma of garlic coming from a simmering pot of spaghetti sauce. "It smells wonderful in here."

Her eyebrows shot up when I handed her the wine and she read the label. "Wow!" she said.

"Can I use your phone?" I asked, nudging K.C., Elizabeth's cat, aside so I could sit down at the galley counter.

"Of course. What's up?"

"I'll tell you in a minute."

I dialed information, asked for the number of the Peninsula Humane Society, and wrote

it on the pad Elizabeth keeps by her phone.
I dialed, and was surprised when someone
actually answered. It was almost 6:00 and I
was afraid they'd be closed for the day.

"My name is Nicoli Hunter," I began,
"I live at a marina on Bair Island Road in
Redwood City where you guys picked up a
big red-haired puppy this afternoon. Do you
know the one I mean?"

"Buddy? Yeah, he's here. Are you the
owner?"

"No, but I really like the dog, and if his
family doesn't claim him I'd like to adopt
him." My heart started pounding as I spoke
the words. A pet is a commitment. What was I
thinking? "Can I give you my phone number,
you know, in case his time runs out?"

The woman took my name and number
and just to be safe I asked for her name as well.
It was Fiona. She wouldn't give me her last
name, but I was pretty sure there wouldn't be
more than one Fiona working at the Humane
Society. I asked her if Buddy had one of those
ID chips implanted in his neck and she said
that he did not.

When I hung up the phone I felt anxious.
I hated the idea of that sweet puppy being
locked in a cage. I hated the idea of *any* dog
being caged.

"What was that all about?" Elizabeth asked, handing me a glass of wine.

"Thanks," I said. "This adorable red-haired dog followed Rocky home. Frank told me he was going to post his picture around the neighborhood to try and find his family, but then he called the Humane Society, and they picked Buddy up today."

"Buddy?"

"That's what Frank named him, because he followed Rocky home, so he was, you know, Rocky's buddy."

"And if nobody claims him you're going to adopt him? Does Bill like dogs?"

"Maybe. I don't know. We haven't talked about it. It doesn't matter anyway. It wouldn't be practical for me to have a dog. I know there are a lot of dogs living on boats here, but I don't think that would work for me. I could adopt him and then find him a home on shore. That way he won't be put to sleep and I'll be able to live with myself."

"He must be some dog."

"He is. He's still a puppy, but his feet are huge so he's going to be big. He has short hair and black markings around his eyes and muzzle, and he's smart. He makes eye contact. Most dogs don't make eye contact. Short hair is good, right?"

DINNER AND A MURDER

"Short hair is very good," she said, smiling indulgently.

I took a sip of the Beaune Cru. Sometimes price does make a difference.

"You know how I feel about dogs," I said. "Speaking of which, have you seen D'Artagnon lately?"

"I know his arthritis is getting worse, if that's what you mean, but I haven't seen him out on deck today."

"Neither have I."

I was wondering if Kirk had decided D'Artagnon was suffering too much, but I didn't want to say it out loud.

Over dinner I filled Elizabeth in on my high school reunion, all the sordid details, including Steve's phone call today. Then I told her about my new case, how I'd asked Sam to help me for the first time since I'd gotten my license, and how worried I was about Paul. She listened to everything I had to say in silence before responding, which is her way, and then told me I was stupid to feel guilty about being attracted to Steve at the reunion. Of course I was no longer attracted to Steve. Steve was pond scum.

"Caring for Bill doesn't mean you're dead, Nikki. It means that when you're attracted to someone else, you don't act on it. You think Bill's never attracted to anyone else?"

That wasn't something I was prepared to contemplate at the moment, what with my current state of nicotine withdrawal.

At the end of the evening I felt lighter, even though I'd eaten my weight in spaghetti and tiramisu. I promised that next time we got together I'd let Elizabeth unload and I would listen.

"I'll look forward to *that*," she said, with an eye roll.

I left around 9:00 and walked slowly past Kirk's boat. D'Artagnon was nowhere in sight, but I was relieved to see that the dog biscuits I had left on the bow were gone.

When I got home I called Bill.

"Do you like dogs?" I asked.

# CHAPTER 11

THERE WAS A MOMENT DURING which I imagined Bill looking at the receiver in confusion.

"Why?" he finally asked.

"There's this big shiny red-haired puppy that followed Rocky home today. He's a shorthair and he has huge feet and big brown eyes and he's adorable, but Frank called the Humane Society and now Buddy's in jail." I took a breath.

"Buddy?" Bill said.

"That's what Frank named him. If nobody claims him and nobody adopts him, you know they'll put him to sleep."

"So, you want to adopt him?"

"Just until I can find him a good home."

"You're a soft touch when it comes to dogs.

Why don't you give it a couple of days, in case his owner is out there looking for him?"

"Sure. Of course. That sounds reasonable." It did sound reasonable, but in the meantime Buddy would be in a cage.

The next morning I tucked my Cyber-shot mini digital camera into my purse, and drove to Burlingame, to the Peninsula Humane Society. I pulled into the parking lot, heard the barking, and instantly felt the pull of all those homeless pups.

I've never noticed that cats have a particular scent, but as I entered the lobby I inhaled the aroma of multiple dogs, and it instantly brought a smile to my face. I was still smiling when I introduced myself to the first employee I spotted, a perky blonde in jeans and a pink polo shirt. Her nametag read Cindy. I asked if Fiona was working today.

"Fiona works in the afternoons," she said. "She's a volunteer."

"I spoke with her last night about a dog that was picked up at a marina in Redwood City yesterday. His name is Buddy. Fiona was going to make a note of my name and phone number in his file, in case no one claims him. I'd like to see him if that's okay."

"I know the dog you mean. Follow me."

Cindy led me through a set of swinging

double doors and out into the area where the dogs were penned. I felt a lump form in my throat as I looked into the eyes of each captive canine.

When we arrived at Buddy's cage I dropped to my knees and put my hand up to the chain-link. He licked my hand through the wire mesh while his roommate, a pit bull terrier, barked and wagged at me. Cindy said she needed to get back to the front desk, and left us alone. Buddy kept licking my hand until I pulled it away and stood to take his picture. Then he sat down and gazed up at the camera lens as though he understood what I was doing. I snapped half a dozen shots through the crosshatching and then put my hand out for more kisses. I promised him that everything was going to be okay, but I could feel my heart breaking as I walked away.

I avoided looking at the other dogs as I moved back toward the office, where I asked Cindy to double check Buddy's file to make sure my name and phone number were listed. They were.

I managed to make it to my car before I started hyperventilating. Bill was right. I am a sucker when it comes to dogs. If I owned a house with sufficient acreage I'd probably rescue every one of them. I drove to the marina fighting the impulse to speed back to the Humane Society and adopt Buddy on the spot.

When I unlocked the office my voicemail light was blinking. I opened the blinds and started a pot of coffee, turned on my computer, and downloaded the pictures I'd taken of Buddy, making enough color copies to post around the marina. Then I listened to my messages. One was from Sam, asking if I had the next of kin information on the accident victims. The other message was from Cher.

I called Cher back first and we made a lunch date for the following Saturday. I gave her directions to the marina and told her I'd meet her at The Diving Pelican.

I hung up the phone and glanced at the fax machine. I had received several pages from Paul. Snatching them up, I made sure they were in numerical sequence, and called Sam.

He picked up on the first ring. "What took you so long?" he said.

"You've got caller ID haven't you, you sneaky bastard? I have the next-of-kin data. Do you want me to scan it to you, fax it to you, read it to you, or bring it to you in person?"

"Fax it to me. I'll call you back when I've looked it over."

I sent the fax, then sat down to read the

pages myself, struggling to focus because the sense of urgency had me a bit rattled. The report included the names, phone numbers, and addresses for the relatives of the deceased accident victims, matched with the names of the family members who had been killed. I was sure this must be privileged information. I hoped Paul wasn't putting his job in jeopardy, but I knew he understood that saving lives was more important than remaining employed.

I automatically focused on the men. I know first-hand that women are capable of killing, but there are fewer female multiple murderers than there are male, so it made sense to look at the men first. Because we'd narrowed the list to those who had lost more than one relative, only three of the names on my list were male. Two had lost a wife and a child, and the third had lost his wife and two children. I shuddered at the thought.

Sam called me back five minutes later.

"Run background checks on the three males," he said. "Regardless of what you find out, we should plan to interview all three of them right away. I need to clear my schedule. Can you do a couple of restaurants for me tonight?"

"Sure. Where do you need me?"

"At the San Leandro Lyons. Ask for a

window booth and order a vegetarian entrée. Do a quick survey of the bar, not more than ten minutes. And make sure you're armed."

Sam was always protective, but in this case he was right. San Leandro is an enchanting little city on the California coast with an extremely high crime rate. Southeast Oakland is right next-door.

"Then what?" I asked.

"Scoma's at Fisherman's Wharf. Ask to be seated in Glen's section. The manager got a complaint about his attitude. See if you can piss him off."

"Okay. Is that it?"

"That's it."

"What time do you want to get together tomorrow?"

"Meet me here at nine a.m. And bring tonight's dinner surveys. We'll take my SUV for the interviews."

I said, "Great," but I was thinking *oh crap!* I hate driving anywhere with Sam. Unless he's tailing someone he drives like an old woman. It's fine to be cautious, but Sam takes defensive driving to the extreme.

I sent an e-mail to CIS, aka Criminal Investigative Services, requesting background checks on each of the three men. I didn't have social security or driver's license numbers, so there was no guarantee I'd get the information I was after. I submitted their names and addresses, including a note saying the backgrounds were urgent and offering a bonus for speed, and hoped for the best.

At 11:00 a.m., I collected my pictures of Buddy and a handful of thumbtacks. I locked up the office and went to The Diving Pelican where I posted one of the pictures on the restaurant's bulletin board. I had added my office telephone number to each photo with a note that said "*Do you know this dog?*"

I posted another picture above the marina mailboxes and then walked around to each of the six gates, tacking photos on all the bulletin boards outside each one. When I was finished I felt a little better, but I still wanted to spring Buddy as soon as possible. I could probably wait a day. Two days tops.

On my way back to the office I stopped at The Diving Pelican again and picked up a newspaper from one of the dispensers Bennet keeps outside for customers. As I walked I scanned the lost and found section of the classified ads. There were several ads for missing dogs, but there was nothing about a red shorthair.

Back at the office I called Bill.

"Anderson," came the expected response.

"Don't you have anything better to do than sit at your desk answering the phone all day?" I asked.

"Hi, Nikki," he said, a smile in his voice.

"How would you feel about doing a couple of restaurant surveys with me tonight? I have to go to Lyons in San Leandro and Scoma's at the Wharf."

"Lyons I can do without, but I'll join you at Scoma's."

"Come for both. Otherwise we'll have to take separate cars. I need to catch the dinner rush at Lyons, so we should probably leave here by six." I checked my watch and was surprised to discover it was already after 12:00.

"I'll try," Bill hedged. "If I'm not there by six, call my cell, and whatever you do don't go to San Leandro without your defense spray."

"Yes sir, Detective Anderson, sir."

"That's right, baby."

As I hung up the phone I pictured myself in a house with a fenced yard and half a dozen dogs. I had to shake myself out of that compelling vision and back into the real world. I stood and walked to the plate glass window overlooking the marina. I could see D'Artagnon lying out on the deck of Kirk's yacht. I had clients who were anxious for their weekly surveys, but I decided there was nothing more important at the moment than taking my friend for a walk, if he was up to it.

I locked the office and jogged down to the dock. I knocked, but no one answered. It was early afternoon on a weekday. Of course, Kirk would be at work. D'Artagnon turned and watched me from the bow. He wagged his tail slowly, but he didn't stand up. My heart moved up into my throat as I approached. I leaned my forehead against his and gently stroked the back of his neck.

"Did you want to go for a walk?" I asked. The tail wagging picked up speed, but he remained lying down. I spent about ten minutes petting the sweet boy and wishing there was something I could do. I walked the short distance to my boat and took a grief-induced nap.

# CHAPTER 12

A T 4:00 P.M. I FORCED myself up off the queen-size bunk, stripped off my clothes, and stepped into the shower.

After blow-drying and scrunching my curls, I dressed in black jeans and a black silk blouse. I tucked my Ruger into the holster at the small of my back and put on my camel hair blazer. I checked my image in the mirror to make sure the silhouette of the gun wasn't visible.

I was hungry, but I knew if I ate anything now I'd be sorry later when I was trying to choke down my second entrée of the evening, so I pocketed half a dozen dog biscuits and headed out. D'Artagnon was no longer on the deck of Kirk's yacht. I knocked on the window and waited, but there was no answer. By the time I reached the office I'd made up my mind that first thing Thursday morning I would adopt Buddy.

I brewed a pot of coffee and was sipping the first cup when the phone rang.

"Hunter Investigations," I answered. There was cell phone static on the line.

"Nikki, it's Kirk. I came home for a late lunch today and D'Artagnon couldn't stand up, so I carried him to the truck and took him to this guy Lily told me about. His name is Bob Culver and he's a chiropractor. I didn't have an appointment, but he managed to squeeze us in. He adjusted D'Artagnon's spine and then he asked me about his diet. He told me to cut out corn, wheat, red meat, sugar, and anything in the nightshade family, like potatoes. I carried D'Artagnon into his office but he walked out on his own. We have to go back a couple times a week, but I think he's going to be okay. I couldn't wait to tell you."

"That's incredible," I said, fighting back tears of relief. "I'm so glad you called."

I typed up some of the surveys I'd done recently and was just completing the invoices when Bill walked in the door at 6:10.

"Do we really have to go to Lyons?" he asked.

"Yes. I'm doing it for Sam because he's helping me with Paul's case."

We took Bill's Mustang and hit the freeway.

On the way to San Leandro he reached for my hand and said, "Nikki, I've been thinking."

"That can't be good," I said, turning to him with a smile.

"Why don't we try living together? See where this takes us. My house has lots of room, and we could still spend some weekends on the boat. Or, if that doesn't appeal to you, maybe I could rent out the house and move aboard with you. We'd have more time together that way."

The smile dropped from my face and I felt a knot form in my solar plexus. "Whoa," I said, snatching my hand away. "Bill, we've only known each other for three months. I really enjoy spending time with you, but don't you think this is rushing things a bit? I don't want to live on land, and if you moved in with me where would you keep your guitars? Plus I only have one hanging locker. Where would we put all your clothes?" While my lips were offering logical arguments against cohabiting on my boat, my lizard brain was screaming, *Oh, hell no!*

I was touched that Bill was willing to sacrifice his comfort in order to have more time with me, but I was not looking for this level of commitment. I preferred living alone.

I needed my privacy and independence, and I treasured the freedom it gave me.

"I do like having all that space," Bill said, "but I think I love you, Nikki." He said it quietly, almost a whisper, then he reached over and gave my hand a gentle squeeze.

Oh *crap*. There it was. The dreaded L word. Were we already moving into that stage of our relationship? I had suspected it was coming eventually, and it made my stomach ache. After my last marriage failed I'd given up on the 'happily ever after' fantasy. Bill had slowly begun changing my mind about that, but this was too much too soon.

"I think I might be falling for you too," I hedged. "But living together just doesn't seem practical to me. I know it's been hard to find time for each other, but I don't think this is the solution. I'm sorry."

There. I'd said it. I hoped my decision wouldn't push Bill away.

"Okay," he said. "No pressure."

No pressure? What did *that* mean? Was he assuming I'd change my mind after I thought about it? I hadn't said I wanted time to think about it, I'd said no. I hate it when men don't listen to me. It's as though they have pre-conceived ideas about what I need, feel, and think, so there's no reason to actually pay attention to the words coming out of my mouth. No pressure my ass! Was I over reacting? I didn't think so.

We were silent for the remainder of the drive.

At 7:20 we pulled into the Lyon's parking lot. We entered the restaurant and waited for the hostess to approach the podium. She was a six-foot tall black woman with her hair pulled up into a bun, which made her look six-two. She was dressed in black slacks, a white blouse, and a red vest. Her nametag read Anna.

"Table for two?" she asked, looking us over.

"Yes," I answered. "We'd really like a window booth, if you have one available."

Anna surveyed the restaurant and said, "Do you mind waiting a few minutes?"

"No problem," I said. "We'll be in the bar."

I could do the bar survey while we waited for a booth to free up. I gave Anna my name and she said she'd come and get us when our table was ready. She was surprisingly professional for a Lyon's hostess.

The bar scene was pretty much what I'd expected. There were a few older couples who had probably lived in San Leandro since the seventies, and there were gang members out on dates with their significant others.

The bartender was Hispanic, about five-eight, with black hair combed straight back and a neatly trimmed mustache. He was dressed in the same uniform of dark slacks, white shirt, and red vest. He was filling a drink order for the cocktail waitress when we entered.

Bill and I took seats at the bar and the bartender approached less than a minute later, placed cocktail napkins in front of us, and nodded deferentially to Bill as though he recognized a cop when he saw one. It wasn't the first time this had happened when I was out with Bill, and I'd learned that the individuals who were adept at spotting police were usually worth watching. His nametag read Hector. I looked at his hands and spotted the tattoos across his knuckles, telling me he'd probably been in prison at some point in his life. From a distance he'd looked maybe thirty-five or forty. Up close he looked fifty. His eyes were dark and revealed a combination of respect and defiance. Interesting mix.

"Two Dos Equis," Bill said, in his tough-guy voice.

What the hell? Since when did Bill order for me? Especially when I was working. He hadn't even asked me what I wanted. This was a new side to the considerate guy I'd spent the last three months dating. He must be one of those men who decide it's time for a commitment and then try to take over your life. I couldn't believe I'd misread him so completely. I mean, I know the balance between people changes when they get married, but prior to tonight we'd never even discussed whether or not we were exclusive. And even if we *were* in a committed relationship I wouldn't want him making decisions for me. This is one of the reasons I choose to live, and work, alone. Nobody can tell me what to do.

Hector placed chilled pilsner glasses on our napkins, then took two bottles of Dos Equis out of the cooler and opened them above the bar. He set the bottles next to the glasses and said, "Twelve dollars."

Bill paid him in cash. Hector recorded the sale and placed a cash register receipt on the bar along with the correct change. Bill left the change on the bar and I picked up the receipt.

The details of what I observed would go into my report but, as always, I would keep any unnecessary opinions to myself. I watched the way Hector cruised the bar, checking on his customers. He smiled and chatted with an elderly couple as he placed fresh napkins under their drinks and refilled the bowl of peanuts in front of them. He was a good bartender. He recorded two other transactions before Anna came and told us our table was ready, and they both looked legitimate to me. Sales were recorded on the register and receipts given to customers.

Anna escorted us to a window booth facing Davis Street. She offered us menus and told us our waitress, Maria, would be right with us. As she departed, Maria approached. She was Caucasian and appeared to be in her late teens, five-six, slender but not anorexic, with brown hair worn in a ponytail, minimal make-up, and a nose piercing. She recited the specials of the day, which included various combinations of protein, carbohydrates, and fat, none of which sounded appetizing. She offered to give us time to consider the menu, but I had another survey to do tonight, and didn't want to wait for her to get back to us.

"What vegetarian entrées to you have?" I asked.

She had turned to walk away and my question caught her mid-stride. To her credit, she only grimaced slightly as she turned back to the table. "We have fettuccini Alfredo and a very nice vegetarian lasagna," she said.

"I'll have the veggie lasagna," I said, turning to Bill.

"Chef Salad with ranch dressing."

I smiled. Both entrées would take only minutes to plate and serve. We could be out of there in half an hour and in San Francisco by 9:00.

While we were waiting to be served I dug my cell phone out of my purse and called Elizabeth.

She answered on the second ring.

"Kirk called me," I began. "He took D'Artagnon to a chiropractor this afternoon. Someone Lily recommended." I told her about the spinal adjustment and dietary changes, and how D'Artagnon had been able to walk again after the adjustment. She was as thrilled as I had been. Everybody loves D'Artagnon.

I ended the call and dropped the phone back into my purse, took a sip of my beer, and looked up at Bill. "Why did you order me a Dos Equis?"

"Because the bartender was Mexican and it's a Mexican beer. I was showing respect."

I stared at him for a moment before I realized he was serious. "Must be a guy thing," I said. "But please don't do that again." I tried to soften my request with a smile, but Bill simply nodded. The dynamics between us were definitely shifting. A relationship that I relied on to be casual and fun was suddenly strained.

Eleven minutes after we ordered, Maria served our entrées. The vegetarian lasagna was predictably bland, but it wasn't over or undercooked and the side vegetables and garnish were fresh and nicely displayed. Five minutes after serving us, Maria returned to ask how everything was. This is one of the things I time. The most professional waiters and waitresses are back within two minutes, giving you just enough time to taste everything, but five minutes is acceptable.

We nibbled at our entrées for ten minutes, and I motioned for the check. At the cash register, Anna recorded the sale and issued a receipt and the correct change. All in all, it was a pretty good survey.

Bill and I were vigilant walking through the parking lot. It was after dark, and you can't be too careful in a city where more than seventy thousand crimes are reported annually.

During the drive to San Francisco Bill appeared to be focused on traffic, but every once in a while he'd reach over and squeeze my hand. Maybe this was his way of apologizing for trying to oh-so-gently bulldoze me into living together, and for ordering the Dos Equis without consulting me first. It was kind of sweet, but I was still irked.

I'd always known that Bill had an authoritarian side. It was a regular source of friction between us, but considering the fact that he apprehends dirt bags for a living I'd accepted it as a necessary part of his persona. Maybe I *was* over reacting. I needed another talk with Elizabeth.

Scoma's was packed. It's a tourist attraction, but also draws the locals because it's at the Wharf, the view is spectacular, the food is fantastic, and the service is usually good.

The hostess gave Bill a quick once-over and then focused on me. She was in her mid-thirties, had brown hair, a pretty face professionally adorned with cosmetics, and intelligent eyes. Her nametag read Shannon.

"Table for two?" she asked me.

"Yes. Is Glen working tonight? My friend told me he was the best." I could only hope that Glen didn't ask who my friend was or I'd be forced to come up with a creative lie. I hate lying, which is unfortunate for someone in my profession.

Shannon looked at a seating chart and asked us to wait a moment. She walked to the dining room entrance and scanned the tables. When she turned back to us she was smiling.

"You're in luck," she said. "There's a table for two available in Glen's section. Follow me, please."

She led us to a small table just to the right of the dining room entrance. She held out my chair for me and then handed each of us a menu and placed a wine list on the table. "Glen will be right with you," she said. "Can I get you something from the bar?"

"That's okay," I said. "We'll wait."

Sam had asked me to try to piss Glen off and I wasn't sure I was up for it after the day I'd had.

"Listen," I whispered to Bill. "I'm supposed to try to make this guy mad, but I really don't feel like a confrontation tonight."

"You want me to be an asshole and see how he reacts?"

"Would you mind?"

"Not at all. I might even enjoy it."

"Thanks."

We were looking at our menus when Glen approached. He was about five-ten, average build, with blond hair, brown eyebrows and mustache, and blue eyes. He appeared to have a slight sneer on his face. I wondered if he might have a cleft palate that caused his upper lip to curl on one side, or maybe a scar. The effect was undeniable. He looked like he was spoiling for a fight.

"Good evening," he said. "My name is Glen and I'll be your server tonight. May I get you something from the bar, or would you like to hear our specials?"

His voice was nasal, as one might expect if

he had a cleft palate, but his eyes were gentle and his tone was soft. I kicked Bill's shin under the table and when his eyes met mine I shook my head slightly, hoping he'd get the message. I wanted to handle this one myself.

"Could I have a single shot of Bombay Sapphire in a rocks glass, straight up and room temperature, please?" I said.

Glen nodded politely and turned to Bill who was trying to control a smirk.

"I'll have a Corona," Bill said. "In the bottle is fine."

"Would you like a lime wedge?"

"Sure."

"I'll be right back," Glen said.

When he'd gone Bill bent over, rubbed his leg and grimaced. "*Ow,*" he said. "Cleft Palate?"

"Probably. It would explain his expression and the nasal quality of his voice. Might also explain a chip on his shoulder, but I haven't seen any evidence of that yet."

"So I can relax and enjoy the show?"

"Yep."

Glen returned and served our drinks. He placed a rocks glass in front of me, and as he turned to set Bill's beer on the table, I took a sip of the gin. I waited until Glen was facing me and then made a show of sniffing my drink. "Are you sure this is Bombay Sapphire?" I asked.

"Yes," he said. "I watched the bartender pour it."

I took another sip. "I don't think it is," I said. "Maybe it's regular Bombay."

"Would you like me to replace the drink?" Glen asked.

I took a third sip, which almost emptied the glass. "I'm sure this isn't Bombay Sapphire," I said.

"I'd be happy to replace the drink," Glen repeated, patiently.

"I don't want to be any trouble, but do you think the bartender would let you bring the bottle to our table, so I could see for myself?"

Glen lifted an eyebrow and said, "I can ask."

When he was gone I turned to Bill and said, "If he comes back with the bottle I'm giving him a thirty percent tip out of my own pocket."

A couple of minutes went by and then, sure enough, Glen came back carrying a tray containing an empty rocks glass and a full, *sealed,* one liter bottle of Bombay Sapphire. He'd somehow convinced the bartender to let him have an unopened bottle so I could break the seal myself. This guy was *good*. He placed a fresh cocktail napkin on the table and put the glass on the napkin, then he set the bottle on the table with the label facing me. I got the point.

"Would you like me to pour?" he asked.

I searched his face for any trace of sarcasm and couldn't find any. "That would be great. Thank you for going to so much trouble."

After he'd poured me a generous shot of the gin, Glen asked, "Would you like to hear tonight's specials?"

He was being so gracious that it almost embarrassed me.

"Yes, thank you," Bill said, and he winked at Glen.

I saw Glen smile and realized they were doing the male bonding thing. Men bond so easily. Women, at least the women I've known, go through a very complex series of tests before deciding whether or not to trust each other. Even when you pass all the tests the bond often remains tentative. My theory is that this has something to do with the female biological urge to reproduce, and with competition for the strong, healthy males. Postmenopausal women are far more trusting.

Glen recited the specials from memory and took our order. He was professional and friendly throughout the evening, and by the

time we were ready to leave I'd decided that if
I surveyed Scoma's again I'd ask for his section
just for the pleasure of being served by him.

My report on Glen would detail all of my
observations, including the physical challenges
he'd apparently overcome. If I ever heard that
he had been let go I would call my cousin
Aaron and ask him to find an attorney to
represent Glen in a wrongful termination suit.
Then I'd call my friend, restaurant owner, and
client, Jessica James, and suggest she hire him
on the spot. I could do these things because
the owner of Scoma's was not my client, he
was Sam's, so, technically, assisting one of
their former employees wouldn't be a conflict
of interest.

When the check came, I paid with a credit
card and left a huge cash tip.

On the way back to the marina Bill made
a few jokes about my performance with the
Bombay Sapphire, but after that he was quiet
until we reached Redwood City. He walked me
to the gate and kissed me soundly, saying he'd
see me soon. I gave him a hug and a smile
before he turned away. I knew I'd hurt his
feelings earlier, but I'd had no choice if I was
going to be honest. I also really appreciated
the fact that he was offering me my space, not

even asking if I'd like overnight company. Or maybe he was he just pissed.

"Thanks for coming with me tonight," I said to his retreating form.

He gave me a wave over his shoulder before climbing back into the Mustang.

I shuffled down the companionway and made the trek to my boat. After stripping off my clothes I climbed into bed and set my Dream Machine for 6:00 a.m., knowing there would be hell to pay if I showed up at Sam's tomorrow without the completed surveys.

# CHAPTER 13

I SLEPT SOUNDLY FOR A CHANGE, and when my Dream Machine went off the next morning I woke up feeling refreshed. I started the coffee going in the galley, then showered onboard and dressed in slacks and a light sweater.

I was in the office by 7:00 checking my e-mail and listening to my voicemail. I spent forty-five minutes typing up Sam's reports on Lyon's and Scoma's, and when I was finished I had the usual feeling of satisfaction, knowing I'd done my job well. I printed two copies of each survey, saved them on a thumb drive, and slipped the drive and the printed copies into an envelope.

I didn't have to be at Sam's for an hour yet, so I returned a few calls and checked my e-mail again. This time I discovered that CIS has sent me the background reports I'd requested on the accident victims' next of kin. I scanned the electronic copies while they were printing. One of the three men had a criminal record— grand theft auto from fifteen years ago—but no assault charges and nothing recent. One had a spousal abuse charge, which had later been dropped, and the third had a clean record. This was good information to have. I checked the addresses and they matched Paul's data. These were my three suspects. I forwarded the e-mail and attachments to Sam. Then I made copies of all the reports and stuffed them in Paul's case file, which I locked in my Pendaflex drawer.

I stopped on my way out the door, walked back to my desk, and removed the Glock twenty-six from its Velcro holster beneath my lap drawer. I used to keep my Ruger under the drawer, but the Glock only weighs twenty ounces. I thought the Velcro would last longer this way. I checked the mag to make sure it was fully loaded and tucked the gun in the holster compartment of my purse.

I let myself into Sam's outer office at 9:02 and was greeted with a booming, "You're late!"

Have I mentioned that Sam is always cranky in the morning?

"Like hell I am!" I shouted in response. "You said nine o'clock. It's nine o'clock!"

"It's nine oh three," he bellowed from his office.

"It's nine oh *two*. Your watch is fast."

I walked into Sam's private office and tossed the envelope with the completed reports and the thumb drive onto his desk.

"Here are your surveys," I said. "The guy at Scoma's doesn't have an attitude problem. He's actually an excellent waiter. He's probably got a cleft palate that alters his facial expression. If they let him go I'll encourage him to sue for wrongful termination. By the way, anytime you need Scoma's done I'd be happy to help out."

Sam glanced at the envelope, then set it aside and focused on the next of kin background reports he'd been studying when I walked in.

"We're going to visit these three subjects today," he said, "and I want you to follow my lead. Don't interject any of your personality. If the shit hits the fan, it would be better if they didn't remember you."

"Why do you think that? This is my case. You're just helping me out, for which I am extremely grateful, by the way."

"Based on the names, I'm guessing the subjects are all Caucasian. If they focus on the old black man they won't be able to pick me out of a group of old black men, but if they focus on you, you might get yourself killed and that would upset me. Good enough reason for you?"

"My first choice would be Gary Boscalo," I commented. "He used to beat his wife."

Sam said nothing as he reread one of the reports. When he'd finished he picked up his coffee, took a sip, set the cup down again, and said, "All right. We'll start with him."

Gary Boscalo was an accountant at Siebel in San Mateo. He'd been there for five years and lived two miles from his work address in a lower middle-class residential neighborhood. Once we were on the road I distracted myself from Sam's driving by reading about Gary. We made it to Siebel in about twenty-five minutes and parked in the visitors' section of the lot. As we entered the lobby Sam took his PI license out of his wallet. He flashed it quickly at the young woman seated behind the reception desk.

"I'm Sam Pettigrew," he said. "I'd appreciate it if you would call Gary Boscalo to the lobby. We're investigating the accident in which his wife and child were killed."

The young woman blanched. Her mouth hung open for a moment, and then she dialed an extension.

"Yeah, Gary?" she said. "Could you come down to the lobby, please? There are some people here investigating your wife's accident. Yeah, from the airline."

It's surprisingly easy to manipulate most people's assumptions.

"He'll be right out," she said to Sam.

He thanked her and we turned away from the reception desk, moving toward the other side of the room. We weren't pretending we were with the airline, but we hadn't corrected her, which might later get us in trouble.

Gary Boscalo barreled into the lobby like a man living on caffeine and adrenaline. He was about five foot nine with thinning brown hair, clean-shaven, and wearing a short-sleeve white shirt, gray slacks, and a red tie. He looked soft around the middle, but his arms were muscular, and his face was grim. I quickly formed the impression that he was a man with a temper.

Sam stepped between us and held out his hand. "Mr. Boscalo?"

Boscalo shook his hand and nodded. "What's this about?"

"We're conducting a follow-up investigation," Sam said. "Just need to ask you a few more questions."

Boscalo let out a sigh and his face relaxed some. "I hope this is the last time," he said. "It's hard reliving the death of your family over and over again. What did you say your name was?"

"Pettigrew," Sam said. "I'm sorry we keep bothering you like this."

"What do you need to know?"

"Would you like to sit down?" Sam asked.

"Is this going to take long? I'm in the middle of a project."

"Only a few minutes," Sam assured him.

We took seats around a coffee table in the lobby.

"I apologize if these are questions you've already answered," Sam began, "We need to know why your wife and daughter were traveling on the date of the accident."

"Why they were traveling? Why the hell do you need to know that?"

"I'm sorry for your loss, Mr. Boscalo. I truly am. We're just trying to be thorough."

Sam was trying to gauge just how flammable Boscalo's temper was. He was intentionally poking at the wound.

Boscalo just sat there for a moment, and then his face collapsed and he started to cry.

He covered his eyes with the heels of his hands and his chest heaved with each sob. We waited it out.

When he had pulled himself together he said, "They were coming back from a visit with my sister-in-law."

Sam asked a series of mundane questions about Boscalo's family life: how often they traveled together, where they went on vacation, things like that. I took notes to justify my presence. When Sam was satisfied with his impression of Boscalo he thanked him politely, apologized again, and we left.

Outside the building I filled my lungs with the cool, fresh air and silently counted my blessings. It's difficult for me to spend time around people who are grieving. I tend to attach myself to their feelings, taking them on as my own.

Our next subject was Martin Wallace, an attorney who worked in Belmont. He had lost his wife and two kids, a boy and a girl. He had no criminal record, but that didn't prove anything. Wallace had a private practice, so he had no partners or associates. That could mean he was independent or it might mean he didn't work and play well with others. I couldn't fault him for that since it's one of the reasons I became a PI.

His office was on El Camino, in an older one-story building. The gold lettering on the glass door read *Martin Wallace, Attorney at Law.* The door was unlocked, so we went inside. A chime sounded softly as the door opened and closed.

There was a small reception area, which was vacant at the moment. Sam approached the desk and was just opening his mouth to speak when a disembodied voice said, "I'll be right with you folks. Just have a seat."

I quickly scanned the ceiling and spotted a surveillance camera. There was an intercom speaker inserted into the wall behind the reception desk. Sam and I exchanged a glance and sat down on a loveseat facing away from the camera.

Wallace left us there for a full five minutes. I timed it. Unless I missed my guess, this guy had control issues. That could be a valuable quality in an attorney, but taken to extremes it could also be dangerous.

When Martin Wallace finally came out to greet us I was surprised by his appearance. He was around five-seven, in his mid-forties, clean-shaven with light brown hair, and about a hundred and eighty-five pounds, with a potbelly. When I think of control freaks I think of self-discipline, and when I think of self-discipline I think of exercise and some degree of self-control at the dinner table. Maybe Wallace had been on a comfort-food binge since losing his wife and kids.

Sam stood up and introduced himself the same way he had with Boscalo, only Wallace didn't take the introduction at face value.

"Are you with the airline?" he asked.

"No," said Sam, with no perceptible hesitation. "We've been asked by the Association of Air Traffic Controllers to conduct an independent investigation." An impressive adlib.

"So, who are you with?" Wallace asked.

Yep. He definitely had control issues.

Sam reached in his pocket and handed Wallace his business card. This was a risky move. If Wallace chose to dig deeper, Sam could be in a lot of trouble. On the other hand, I knew Paul would back us up if push came to shove.

Wallace took the proffered card and stared at it for a moment. A hint of a smile played over his face and then vanished. "What would you like to know?" he asked.

Sam repeated the questions he'd asked Boscalo, including the one about why his wife and children were traveling on the day of the accident. I recorded Wallace's answers in my notebook. He spoke with no emotion whatsoever, but as Sam continued to question him a sheen of perspiration appeared on his face. He occasionally looked my way, but seemed to concentrate primarily on Sam. That suited me fine because this guy was creeping me out.

When Sam was finished he thanked Wallace for his time and said he was sorry for his loss. It was the only time Wallace's expression changed. He pursed his lips as though he was trying to stop something from bursting out of his mouth. His face flushed and his hands clenched into fists. For an instant I thought he was going to hit Sam. It was pretty intense. Then he straightened his tie and said, "Thank you."

We left the office as casually as we had entered. Neither of us said a word as we walked to the Range Rover. Sam beeped the locks open and we got in. He started the engine and pulled away from the curb.

When we were about a block away I let out the breath I'd been holding and said, "What the hell was that?"

"You noticed it too?"

"He's on the edge."

"Just lost his wife and two kids. Makes sense he'd be upset. What doesn't make sense is that he would control it so completely until someone says they're sorry for his loss. That man's an assault looking for a place to happen."

"No history of violence," I said.

"No history of any *arrests* for violence," Sam corrected me. "Doesn't mean he has no history of violence. Just means he never got arrested for it."

"He's an attorney," I said.

"So he's probably used to being careful about his image. I'd like to take a closer look."

We moved on to interview number three, Charles aka Chuck Fragoso. Fragoso was a department manager at Best Buy in San Carlos. He'd been arrested fifteen years earlier for grand theft auto, had served two years, and then was on parole for another eighteen months. I knew why Sam had saved Fragoso for last. He had the lowest level of education of the three. Although that didn't necessarily mean he was the least intelligent, the odds were against him being our killer. The person who was targeting air traffic controllers had done some research, planning, stalking, and calculated risk taking. We were looking for a psycho with a high IQ.

Sam parked the Range Rover in the Best Buy lot and said, "You're buying me lunch after this."

"Great. I'm starved. How about The Diving Pelican at the marina?"

"Fine with me."

We entered the store and looked around for home entertainment, Fragoso's department. We located a customer service kiosk and an elderly woman dressed in a royal blue smock gave us directions.

Chuck Fragoso was thirty-eight, six-one, lean, and wiry. He had dark hair and eyes, a mustache and goatee, and a small silver hoop in his left earlobe. He was wearing brown slacks with a white short-sleeve shirt and a purple paisley tie.

As we approached, he was discussing the merits of a plasma screen TV with a young couple. I wondered how anyone who wasn't at work on a Wednesday afternoon could afford a plasma screen. Maybe they were on their lunch break. The couple decided to think about the purchase and wandered off, whispering to each other.

I hung back as I had with the other two subjects while Sam approached Fragoso, introduced himself, and asked if there was some place we could speak privately.

"I guess I could take a break," Fragoso said.

He excused himself and walked over to an adjacent department, apparently asking someone to cover for him while he was gone. Then we all trooped outside to the parking lot. Fragoso led us around the side of the building to a picnic table. He lit a cigarette and sat down.

"So you're still investigating the crash?" he asked. "How long does it usually take to sort these things out?"

"Depends on the circumstances," Sam answered equitably.

"How can I help?" Fragoso asked.

Sam began the same litany of questions, but I noticed he was making more eye contact with Fragoso than he had with the other two men. When he asked about why Mindy and their daughter, Samantha, had been traveling on that fateful day, I saw Fragoso flinch.

After a moment, he quietly said, "They were coming back to me."

"Coming back?" Sam pressed.

"Mindy took Samantha and left me nine months ago. She moved to Seattle to stay with her folks. We were talking a couple of times a week and we were working things out. They were coming back to me." His face flushed and his eyes filled with tears.

"I'm sorry," Sam said.

Fragoso rested his forehead in his hands

for a minute and then swiped at the tears. "What else do you need to know?" he asked.

"I think we've taken enough of your time for today," Sam said. "Can we call you if we think of any other questions?"

"Sure." Fragoso produced his business card and Sam accepted it.

We left the Best Buy lot and Sam drove to the marina without asking for directions. I raised a mental eyebrow. I wondered if he'd been there before, maybe checking up on me.

"You come here often?" I asked.

"Been out this way once or twice," he said.

He parked in the side lot nearest the restaurant and we entered The Diving Pelican, both of us automatically turning toward the specials posted on a chalkboard. I decided on the Chinese chicken salad and approached the counter to place my order. Sam followed me and requested the meatloaf. Anyone who's spent time at The Pelican knows the meatloaf is sublime.

After I'd paid for our meals, we poured ourselves ice water, grabbed napkins and flatware, and chose a table on the outdoor deck facing the water. Sam took an ashtray from one of the other tables, lit a cigar, and leaned back in his chair, looking out at the boats.

"This is where you live?" he asked, casually.

I suddenly felt guilty as hell that I'd never invited Sam to my home or even to my office. I pointed out my boat and said, "That one is mine. I'll give you a tour after lunch."

I was suddenly apprehensive. I was sure there were piles of clothes on the stateroom floor and I couldn't remember if I'd washed the morning dishes. *Shit!*

"No need for that," Sam said, shifting his gaze to the right, looking directly at my office.

"I'll show you my office while we're at it," I said. "It's on the way to the boat."

I *knew* the office was a mess. The real question was, why did I care? Sam's office was sloppy too. He probably wouldn't even notice. Maybe on some level I wanted to impress him.

I was thoroughly confused about what I should be feeling by the time Bennett delivered our lunch.

"Well, Ms. Hunter," he said. "I haven't seen much of you lately."

"I'm here at least twice a week. I've just been missing you. Bennett, this is my friend and mentor Sam Pettigrew. Bennett is the owner of this fine establishment," I said to Sam.

They shook hands and I thought I saw recognition in Bennett's expression. Why would Sam come to the marina for lunch and not drop in to see me? Maybe he was waiting for an invitation. But that would mean he was insecure and vulnerable, like a normal person. Sam Pettigrew is *not* a normal person.

We talked about the case over lunch. All three subjects had reason to seek revenge, having lost their wives and children. What we needed to figure out was if any of them had enough rage and was amoral enough to kill. We would have to interview their friends and neighbors as well as conducting surveillance on our three subjects. Not an easy task, considering there were only two of us and we both had other clients. Time was an issue. Sam suggested we each take one of the three, and share the third.

I drew the short straw and ended up with Wallace, the attorney. Of the three, he bothered me the most. Sam chose Fragoso, the manager at Best Buy, and we would work on Boscalo, the accountant, together.

"If we don't get anything useful from watching these three and interviewing their friends and neighbors," said Sam, "we'll take a look at the other families of the deceased passengers and flight crew members."

After lunch we crossed the marina to my office. I took a deep breath as I unlocked the door. There were stacks of file folders all over the desk. I knew what was in each of the piles but they looked disorderly and I didn't like Sam seeing them. I proudly showed him my kitchenette, my closet, and my bathroom.

As we walked through each room Sam murmured, "Very nice." He was being polite, which was totally out of character for him.

While Sam was using my restroom I took the Glock out of my purse and put it back in its holster under my desk.

The office tour had gone surprisingly well, but I didn't know how Sam would react to the boat. It's been my experience that a lot of people don't understand the concept of living aboard. The quarters are cramped and the movement of the boat can feel unstable if you don't have sea legs, but for me it's all about freedom. Knowing I can untie the lines and take off anytime I want.

I locked up the office and we walked down to the dock. When we reached my slip I stopped and announced, "This is *Turning Point*." The Cheoy Lee's cockpit pilothouse doubles as my enclosed front porch up on deck. It's where I enter and also where the steering console is housed. From the pilothouse you descend a companionway which takes you down into the galley, which, in turn, exits aft into the stateroom, and forward into the main salon where I spend most of my time—it's my living room. The aft stateroom is my bedroom. It has built-in drawers surrounding the queen-size bunk, and a single hanging locker or closet. Like I said—close quarters.

Sam ran his hand almost affectionately over the Cheoy Lee's mahogany brightwork, then climbed aboard without hesitation. When he entered the pilothouse, he rested his hand on the wheel, and I could tell he was imagining what it would be like to take her out.

"Have you ever been sailing?" I asked.

"Not in a long time," he said wistfully.

"Jeez, Sam. I didn't know you liked to sail. We should go out sometime. After we crack this case why don't we take her out for a spin?"

He turned and looked at me quizzically. "I'm a little old for sailing," he said.

"No you're not. You're healthy and your balance is good. Of course, if you don't want to go."

"I'd like to go sailing, Nicoli. But it's been a while."

"It'll come back to you," I said.

I felt myself mellowing toward Sam. If we went sailing together I'd probably never look at him the same way again. He would no longer be the great and powerful Oz. Maybe that wasn't such a bad thing.

Sam backed down the companionway and his gaze fell on the miniature maple tree in the antique pot sitting on my galley counter. He had given it to me when I got my PI license and left his employ.

"I don't know what possessed me to give you that plant," he said. "I guess I thought it would do you good to have something to take care of. I never expected it to live this long."

"I didn't think it would either," I said. "But I'm glad it did."

That was a half-truth. I resented the time I spent trimming, watering, and turning the thing so it got even light. I'd tried to palm it off on my mom, my ex-husband, and a few of my friends and neighbors, but all my neighbors live aboard and plants get banged up when you're underway.

After touring my boat, we drove back to Sam's office and plotted out the afternoon. I'd start by interviewing Wallace's neighbors. Sam would spend his afternoon canvassing the apartment complex where Fragoso lived. He'd speak with the building manager first and then move on to the neighbors nearest Fragoso's unit, working his way around the complex. We would get together tomorrow at noon to discuss what we had learned and move on to Boscalo. Sam had regular customers he needed to take care of tomorrow, and first thing in the morning I was going for Buddy. I didn't want the pup to be stuck in the car all day, so I'd have to arrange for someone at the marina to spend the afternoon with him.

# CHAPTER 14

A s I LEFT SAM'S OFFICE I pulled out my cell and called Elizabeth. She answered after one ring, her voice cheerful.

"I need a huge favor," I began.

"What's up?"

"I'm adopting Buddy tomorrow morning and I have to work all afternoon. I don't want to leave him alone in my car or on the boat after he's been locked in a cage for three days, so I was wondering," I took a breath and rushed on, "Could you possibly take tomorrow afternoon off and walk him around the marina, you know, introduce him to the place and make him feel welcome while I pursue the evil forces of the universe and try to save our fragile planet from harm?"

"Okay, that last part was over the top, but I'd be happy to help out. I'll take a personal day. In fact I can leave work now if you want to pick him up this afternoon. I'd like to be there with you when you adopt him."

"That would be great. But I can't do it today. I have a bunch of interviews to conduct on Paul's case."

"What time are you leaving?"

"You mean what time am I starting the interviews? Um, now."

"I'll be at your office in fifteen minutes," and she hung up.

I looked at my cell phone wondering what had just happened, but not unhappy about it.

I made it back to the office five minutes before Elizabeth breezed in at 1:15. I gave her a quick hug, grabbed my shoulder bag, and escorted her back outside and into my BMW.

Wallace lived in the Belmont Hills. Most of the lots there were large, so neighbors could potentially be separated by an acre or two, but you never knew what people might see or hear, and it was important to check everything.

"I'm glad you're coming with me," I said. "These interviews will go faster with you along."

Elizabeth is an expert at wheedling information out of people.

As we drove to Wallace's address I told her that Bill had suggested we try living together.

"How do you feel about that?"

"I think it's a bad idea. I'm crazy about Bill, most of the time, but I'm not looking for a commitment. Not that big of a commitment anyway. Living together usually leads to marriage, and I don't want to be married. I like things the way they are."

"Did you tell him that?"

"Pretty much."

"And what did he say?"

"He said he thinks he loves me."

"Oh. Well, love is good. Do you love him?"

"I don't know. Maybe."

"Do you think this is a deal breaker for him?"

"I hope not. He really is a great guy. A little controlling sometimes, but he's a cop, so I guess that's to be expected. I'm afraid that moving in together would make him feel like he had a right to, I don't know, dominate the relationship. Anyway, he asked, and I said no. I guess I'll have to wait and see what happens next."

We put our conversation on hold as I pulled to the curb across the street from Wallace's house. He lived in a peach-colored, two-story Mediterranean that looked freshly painted. The landscaping was pristine. I grabbed my Cyber-shot, and snapped a few quick pictures

of the house. I checked to make sure the tape
recorder in my purse was set on voice activate
and pulled a clipboard out of the trunk, along
with a short stack of generic forms which
allow me to look official regardless of what
I'm doing.

What I always hope for when I'm conducting
neighbor interviews is a housekeeper who is
home alone, bored, and nosey. Some of my
best sources have been domestics.

Elizabeth and I stood on the sidewalk,
scoping out the neighborhood. There was an
old, faded yellow VW Bug parked in front
of the house to the left of Wallace's. Either
it was an employee's vehicle or someone's
teenager was home from school on a weekday.
We spotted it at the same time, looked at each
other, and headed down the long driveway.

Elizabeth rang the doorbell and then
stepped back. I reached inside my purse
and positioned the tape recorder with the
microphone facing the top of the bag. After a
few moments the door was opened by a woman
in her late forties. Her dark hair was pulled
back in a ponytail at the nape of her neck. She
was solid-looking, her posture was perfect,
and her brown eyes were assessing. She wore a
cream-colored sweat-suit, white Reeboks, and
coral lipstick.

"Good afternoon," I began. "Sorry to bother you. Are you the owner of the house?"

"No," She replied. "She's at work."

"We were hoping to speak with someone who spends a lot of time here in the neighborhood."

She raised an eyebrow. "What's this about?"

"We're conducting an investigation," I said. "We have some questions about the family next door."

I didn't mention the name, but she leaned out the door and glanced to her left, at Wallace's house. "You'd better come inside," she said.

We stepped into the foyer and introduced ourselves. Her name was Gina Cirone. Once the introductions were out of the way, Gina asked if we wanted coffee.

"Please," I said.

"I'd love some," Elizabeth chirped. Elizabeth doesn't normally drink coffee, but she is always gracious.

I was hoping Gina would offer something more substantial since I was presently missing nicotine more than usual and needed a substitute vice. I was in luck. She produced a plate of fresh baked cheese scones and blueberry muffins. As we sat companionably around the cozy kitchen table, looking out on the lavish backyard, drinking French roast coffee and eating scones and muffins, Gina told us she had been Carmen Murillo's housekeeper for the last four years. She was comfortable with the routine, but it wasn't very stimulating. Perfect.

"So, Gina," I began. "We need to know anything you can tell us about the Wallace family."

I let the statement hang. Usually a subject will start talking just to fill the silence. Most people are uncomfortable with silence. Gina was no exception.

"They were quiet," she said. "The wife and kids, I mean. Kept to themselves. Carmen invited them to her Christmas party every year. The wife was pretty, but timid. She almost never spoke. I think she was afraid of saying the wrong thing. The children were very well behaved and very well dressed. They were quiet too. Mr. Wallace was the most talkative one in that family."

"Did you ever see Mrs. Wallace apart from Mr. Wallace?" Elizabeth asked.

"Just in the driveway. She would drive the kids to school, and when she came home she'd park the SUV in the driveway instead of putting it in the garage. Sometimes I'd see her when she came home with the groceries."

"Did they have live-in help?" I asked.

"No, but someone comes in to clean twice a week."

We talked with Gina for twenty minutes. The most relevant piece of information she had to offer was that she didn't like Wallace. I didn't like Wallace either. That didn't make him a killer, but I would look extra hard at him because of it.

Before we left, I asked if she could introduce us to any of the other employees in the neighborhood. She walked us next door to a stately two-story brick house, took us to a side door, and entered the kitchen without knocking.

"Ethel?" she called out, as she entered.

A pink-faced, silver-haired woman in a crisp white uniform popped up from behind a granite center island. "Gina! What a nice surprise. Who are your friends?"

Gina introduced us to Ethel MacDougall, cook and housekeeper to Mr. and Mrs. Abernathy. The four of us sat down at the kitchen table and Ethel served everyone coffee cake. I accepted a small piece, but I'd already eaten two of Gina's cheese scones and I knew the carbs were going to give me a headache. Everything has a price.

Ethel insisted she knew less about the

Wallaces than Gina did, being one house further removed, however she did say she had observed the mister in the driveway one night slapping the missus. She didn't know what had provoked the attack, only that the missus was crying at the time. Ethel said she had barely controlled her desire to take a frying pan to his skull.

Both Elizabeth and I used the bathroom off Ethel's kitchen before moving on. We asked if either of them could introduce us to anyone else in the neighborhood, and Ethel picked up the phone.

Our next stop was the house across the street from Wallace's. The driveways were long, but if you stood in the middle of the street between the two houses you could see in both front windows, which were directly across from each other. This house was a Tudor with beautifully manicured grounds and a fire engine red front door. The brass knocker was in the shape of a boar's head. I couldn't resist using it. After about thirty seconds the door was answered by a young woman wearing white shorts and a powder-blue tank top. Her skin was the color of cappuccino and her smile displayed a perfect set of brilliant white teeth. In fact, everything about her appeared to be perfect. She was at least five-ten in her Nikes, and maybe a hundred and forty-five pounds of lean body mass.

"Hi," I said. "We're looking for Rebecca."

"I'm Rebecca," said the young goddess. "You must be Nicoli and Elizabeth. Ethel said you'd be right over. Come on in."

We entered the house and I looked around, hoping to find a layer of dust on the furniture, a smudge on a mirror, dirt on the carpet or scratches on the hardwood floor, but there was nothing. She was beautiful *and* efficient. Not much potential for likeability.

Rebecca ushered us into the living room. Willow trees framed the floor-to-ceiling windows and an ebony baby grand piano sat in the corner, surrounded by bookshelves filled with sheet music. I wondered if the owner of the house was a concert pianist.

"Did Ethel tell you why we're here?" Elizabeth asked.

"She said you were asking about Wallace." I thought I detected a slight shudder when she said his name.

"That's right," I said. "We're doing background research on the victims of the accident that killed his wife and children."

"Oh," she said, sounding disappointed. "Why are you researching the victims' backgrounds?"

I looked into her shrewd brown eyes and wondered why she was working as a domestic. "What's your major?" I asked, taking a shot.

"Political Science at the moment. I'm pre-law," she said.

*Of course.* "Night classes?"

"Some day classes too. I live in, so I can work whenever I'm not in class."

"That must be nice," I said. I was thinking maybe Rebecca took care of more than the house and mentally slapped myself for the assumption.

"Are you going to answer my question?" she asked.

"Sorry," I said. "You're the first person who's asked. We're researching the background of each passenger to determine their life insurance value for any potential law suits. Not everyone buys preflight insurance."

It was a good lie. One I'd spent a lot of time thinking up. I was proud of it, and thought I had delivered it convincingly.

"I guess that makes sense. Mind if I look at your credentials?"

"Not at all."

I took out my wallet, showed her my PI license, and handed her one of my business cards. She accepted the card and read the license carefully. Then she looked at Elizabeth expectantly.

"Elizabeth is my associate," I said. "If you'd rather not talk to us, that's okay."

"I don't mind talking to you. I just wanted to be sure you weren't working for that asshole across the street." She waved her hand in the direction of Wallace's house. Now we were getting somewhere.

"That's reassuring," I said. "I was wondering if it was just me."

"You've met him?" she asked, looking suspicious again.

"Yesterday," I said. "Totally anal."

"He's a peeping-Tom," she said. "You want coffee or something?"

"No, thanks. We're pretty much coffeed out," said Elizabeth. "So Wallace has been watching you? Like, with binoculars?"

She shook her head. "Camera. He's got a telephoto lens."

"What can you tell us about his wife?" I asked. "Did she seem to be afraid of him?"

"Any rational person would be afraid of him. I don't like to judge people," she said, with a self-deprecating smile. "I know it sounds like I'm really into putting him down, but that's not my style. I almost quit my job because of that man."

"How did he treat his wife and kids?" Elizabeth asked, trying to steer her back to the reason for our visit.

"I saw him hit her a couple of times, and he used to yell at her a lot. I've read about people like him. They feel threatened by anything they can't control."

"You're very observant," I said. "What else have you seen him doing?"

"You mean besides watching me with his camera?" I nodded. "My boss, David, and I went to Carmen's Christmas party together the last two years, and at both parties Wallace stared at me the whole time he was there, even though his wife was standing right next to him. I could feel his eyes on me the minute he walked in. It's creepy. Almost like being stalked. When he's watching me with the camera I can feel it. I turn around and there he is. And he doesn't stop when he knows I see what he's doing. Can you believe that?"

"Maybe he wants you to know," Elizabeth ventured.

"I thought voyeurism was about being sneaky. You think it turns him on that I know he's watching me?" She covered her throat with her hand and looked like she might be sick.

"It might," I said. "He may want you to

feel that he can exert power over you, even from a distance."

"That's disgusting," Rebecca said. "So what can I tell you that will get him out of my life?"

I raised an eyebrow and said nothing.

"Oh come on. You're not investigating the victims of a plane crash. You're looking at Wallace for some other reason and whatever it is, I'm in."

I wondered if she was volunteering to lie on the witness stand to get rid of a nasty neighbor.

"We really are conducting background investigations on the victims of the crash," I said. "What we need from you is information about the relationship between Wallace and his wife and kids. Anything you observed first-hand, or overheard."

She sighed. "If you say so. I'm naturally skeptical. Probably got it from my dad. He was a cop, killed in the line of duty. If he was still alive all I'd have to do is ask him to talk to Wallace. Dad had a way of talking to people so they understood it was in their best interest to do the right thing.

"What I observed about Wallace's relationship with his wife and kids was that he didn't respect them. He treated them like property. He talked down to his wife. Told her what to do, and she did it. I never heard his kids speak in his presence, but they were pretty chatty with their mom when he wasn't around. Sometimes I would be out in the front yard gardening when they got home from school, and I'd hear them telling her all about their day.

"On the few occasions when they'd all go out together the kids were like zombies—silent and obedient. I saw him slap his wife's face once, in the driveway. And I saw him punch her in the face one time, in the front room. I was getting into my car to go to class and I heard him shouting, so I looked across the street. I never saw him hit the kids, but he probably knocked them around too."

"Has his behavior changed since the accident?" I asked. "Have you noticed him leaving the house late at night or very early in the morning?" I knew I was tipping my hand, but it was information I needed.

Rebecca stared at me for a moment. "No," she finally said, "but I usually go to bed around ten and I'm a sound sleeper, so if he went out late I wouldn't know."

I rose to leave and Rebecca held up a hand. "Wait," she said. "You're a PI, right?" I nodded, wondering where this was going.

"Could I hire you to install some video surveillance equipment?"

"I suppose so. What do you want to keep an eye on?"

"Wallace," she said. "I want evidence that he's a pervert. I want to get him on film watching me with his nasty little camera. He probably jacks off while he's doing it." She shuddered.

"I can't install the equipment on his property, but if it's okay with your employer, I can install it in one of the rooms facing Wallace's house. Will that work?"

"I think so," she said, smiling now. "How much will it cost?"

"I can get the equipment for about fifteen hundred. I'll throw in the labor for free if you let me watch the videos."

"Deal," she said, and reached out to shake my hand.

I took her hand and she wrapped her other arm around me and hugged me. It took me by surprise. I guess she was grateful to have an ally in the battle against Wallace. So was I.

"I can't do it today," I said into her shoulder, "but maybe I can come by on Monday while Wallace is at work."

"Monday's good," she said. "That'll give me time to explain the situation to David."

Before Elizabeth and I left, I gave Rebecca my home and cell phone numbers and asked her to call if anything unusual happened. I didn't know what that might be, but I had a feeling she would call. I asked for her phone number and entered it in my cell.

Elizabeth and I knocked on a couple more doors, but didn't gather any new intel. I was satisfied that Wallace was a monster. I just didn't know yet what level of monster he was.

We drove back to the marina in silence, probably because we were both contemplating what Rebecca had shared with us about Wallace and his perversions. I parked in the boat owner's lot and turned to Elizabeth. "Thanks for helping with the interviews," I said.

"It was fun. What time are we leaving for the Humane Society in the morning?"

"I'm not sure when they open, but I'd like to get there early."

"Okay," she said. "Come over for breakfast."

She headed for the docks and her trawler, and I went back to the office.

I started a pot of coffee and cleared everything off my desk. I didn't want anything to distract me. I even closed the blinds so the view of the marina wouldn't divert my attention. I stacked the accident reports in the middle of my desk, poured a mugful of coffee, and sat down. I wished briefly for a cigarette, remembering how the nicotine used to help me focus, but caffeine would have to be enough for now.

I dug through the pages and eventually found the accident that had caused Wallace, Fragoso, and Boscalo to lose their wives and children. I copied the individual pages and reinserted the originals back into the stack so I'd have a complete set in sequence. I spent the rest of my afternoon reading through the accident report to get a better handle on what had caused the plane crash that had taken the lives of our subjects' families. I'm a visual person. I needed to picture the tragedy in order to understand how each individual might be reacting to his loss.

The plane crash had occurred on August 16th at 3:05 a.m. Pacific Standard time. The air traffic controller had radioed the pilot at 2:58 a.m., instructing him to correct his trajectory. The angle was too steep and the aircraft was coming in slightly off course. The pilot had not responded to the ATC's warning, and the aircraft had subsequently crashed into a field near SFO, killing everyone onboard.

The team investigating the incident suspected that the pilot and co-pilot were unconscious at the time of the crash. Carbon monoxide poisoning was suggested as one possible cause. The investigation was ongoing, but there was no indication of incompetence or neglect on the part of the pilot or the controller.

I highlighted the relevant passages and then summarized them in a Word document, which I printed and stowed in the file I was building for Paul. A quick look at my watch told me I could catch him at home if I called now. He needed to know what was happening with the investigation, and I needed to know that he was okay. It had been five days since the last controller, Gordon Mayes, had been killed.

Paul answered on the second ring.

"Hi, Nikki."

He sounded defeated, or maybe just exhausted. It must be hard enough to sleep during the day without worrying about whether or not a homicidal maniac was waiting to pick you off.

"Hi, Paul. I wanted to give you an update on what Sam and I have been doing."

I filled him in on the background data we'd collected so far on Wallace, Fragoso, and Boscalo. I explained why we'd chosen to focus on these three individuals, and told him about interviewing each of them this morning and Wallace's neighbors this afternoon. Paul silently took it all in. I could almost feel his desperation through the phone line.

"How are you doing, Paul?"

"I've been better. So you think the killer was related to someone onboard the August 16th flight?"

"That's our supposition, since it was the only recent accident with fatalities. Have you said anything to the other controllers who report to you?"

"There are only two left at SFO who were working the morning of that crash. Besides me, I mean. Arthur Mann and Kim List. They know about what happened to James, Shirley, and Gordon. There's a lot of speculation going on over coffee in the break room. I'm not the only one convinced these deaths weren't accidental."

What neither of us said was that Paul *was* the only one who would feel responsible if another member of his staff was killed.

"Maybe you should all hire body guards," I said, "speaking of which, have you called Quinn yet?"

"No, not yet."

"You know, Paul, the time to hire a bodyguard is *before* you need one."

Paul promised he would think about it, and we ended the call.

I was starting to have trouble focusing, so I poured another mug of coffee. I cracked the blinds and looked down at Kirk and D'Artagnon's boat. Then I remembered that I was adopting Buddy in the morning. Even if I only kept him until I found him a better home, at least he'd be mine for a while. The thought made me smile.

# CHAPTER 15

As PAUL MARKS DROVE TO work that night he was unaware that he was being shadowed. The killer followed him from his home in San Mateo all the way to SFO, mentally recording his route, and noting where he parked his BMW Z4 in the gated lot. He used binoculars to watch as Marks locked his car and scanned the area nervously, then crossed to the secure tower building.

The killer pulled back onto the frontage road and drove to his own 'secure building', relishing the anticipation of his next objective.

# CHAPTER 16

WHEN MY DREAM MACHINE WOKE me on Thursday morning the first thing I thought of was Buddy. It was a surprisingly happy thought, considering how I'd avoided having a pet since the loss of my English Mastiff three years ago.

I hadn't slept well the night before, in spite of exhausting myself reading and summarizing the accident report. I brewed a pot of Kona and sat at the galley counter wondering if my sailboat would be too confining for a big dog. Rocky seemed okay on Frank's boat. Of course, I couldn't leave Buddy alone while I was working. Dogs are pack animals, and he'd probably develop separation anxiety and eat the settee cushions or something. I wondered if he was still teething. The woman at the pound had said he was about six months old. I'd have to get him some chew toys.

I realized I was thinking of Buddy as mine—thinking long term. I'd posted the photos of him around the marina two days ago and no one had called yet. What if his family had already claimed him? I hadn't been to the pound since Tuesday. The realization that he might be gone shocked me. I'd assumed that he would be waiting for me to come and get him. I glanced at my watch. It was 6:15.

Thirty minutes later I was showered and dressed and knocking on Elizabeth's door. She slid it open and squinted out at the daylight. "It's early," she said.

"I know. Sorry. I want to be there when they open."

Her jaw dropped. "Oh my *God*," she said. "You're afraid someone else is going to adopt him, aren't you?"

"Shut up."

She grinned at me. "Come inside while I get dressed."

I climbed the dock steps, went inside, and closed the door behind me.

"I haven't made breakfast yet," Elizabeth called out from the stateroom. "Are you hungry?"

"A little. But we can eat after we pick him up."

"You are so funny," she said.

"Shut *up!*"

I heard soft chuckling coming from the stateroom as I paced around the galley. I was in a hurry to get to the Humane Society, which probably wouldn't be open for at least another hour.

We arrived in Burlingame at 7:30. The sign on the locked door stated that adoption hours were from 11:00 a.m. to 7:00 p.m.

"*Crap!*" I shouted, apparently loud enough to start the dogs barking. I wondered if Buddy recognized my voice. I peered through the glass doors, hoping there might be a benevolent employee inside who would allow me to adopt outside of the posted hours. I didn't see anyone, and the lights weren't on. *Crap, crap, crap!*

"What do you want to do?" Elizabeth asked.

"Let's head over to Burlingame Avenue and grab some breakfast. They should be open by the time we get back. Maybe I can convince them to let me adopt Buddy before eleven. I have to meet Sam at twelve."

We settled on Alana's Café, which opened at 7:00. A window table was available, so we dropped our purses and jackets, then I snagged menus from the waitress behind the counter. I ordered scrambled eggs with shrimp, and coffee, of course. Elizabeth requested a Swiss cheese and mushroom omelet. The food at Alana's was good, the prices reasonable, and the atmosphere friendly. I tried to relax and enjoy my breakfast, but I was anxious both about the adoption and about getting back to work on Paul's case.

We pulled into the Humane Society lot at 8:45. The doors were now unlocked and the overhead lights were on. There was a petite blonde woman behind the counter. Her nametag read Karen. She wore her hair in a ponytail and was dressed in a pink polo shirt and tan jeans.

"I'm here to adopt Buddy," I blurted out, as soon as I was inside. "My name is Nicoli Hunter. I called the day he was brought in and left my name and number in case his family didn't claim him. Is he still here?"

Elizabeth put her hand on my shoulder and said, "Breathe."

"Yeah, he's here," Karen said, smiling. "You need to fill out some paperwork. We can get the process started, but you'll have to come back after eleven to pick him up."

"I'd really appreciate it if you would let me complete the process and take him with me this morning. I have an appointment at 12:00 today."

Karen gave me a clipboard with a short stack of forms and a pen, then said, "I'm sorry, but our policy is to only allow adoptions between eleven and seven. Maybe you can come back after your appointment."

I stood at the counter to fill out the forms, not wanting anyone to get in line ahead of me. I rushed through the paperwork, slowing when I got to the section that asked about my living situation. I didn't imagine many of the individuals adopting dogs lived aboard boats. I didn't want to risk being turned down for the adoption, but I didn't want to lie either. I listed the Cheoy Lee's dimensions and included information about the wildlife refuge across the street and the park-like grounds of the marina. I also noted the many other dogs who lived aboard who would be Buddy's friends, and my neighbors who would look after him when I was unable to be at home or to have him with me while I was working.

When I was finished I handed the forms back to Karen and she called someone to bring Buddy inside. She asked us to wait in a small room just off the lobby, saying she wanted to ask me a few questions and observe my interaction with the dog. I'd had no idea the Humane Society was so thorough. It was reassuring to know that they wouldn't give a dog to just anyone who walked in off the street.

The room in which we were seated was equipped with three white plastic chairs, two tennis balls, a rope chew toy, and a blue beanbag chair. We waited a couple of minutes before Karen brought Buddy in on a green nylon leash. I noticed immediately that his demeanor had changed since I'd first met him. His tail was between his legs and his head was held low, as though he was afraid of being hit. It broke my heart to see him like this. Then he raised his eyes and saw me, or maybe he smelled me. His head came up and his tail started wagging frantically. A sound I can only describe as a moan escaped his lips as he strained against the leash. Karen let go and Buddy launched himself into my lap. I started laughing but there were tears in my eyes. I couldn't help it. I hugged him and he licked my hands and face and then burrowed under my arm with a sigh.

Elizabeth pulled a tissue out of her purse and handed it to me.

Karen asked me questions about my job and my living situation, how often I would walk Buddy, and what I planned to feed him. She gave me tags for his collar, and I let her install one of those electronic chips between his shoulder blades, so if the license on his collar came off any vet could scan him like a grocery item and access my name, address, and phone number. I looked over Buddy's paperwork while Karen was injecting the chip. Apparently the Humane Society vet had decided he was a mixture of Golden Retriever and Rhodesian Ridgeback.

After I'd paid the fee Elizabeth and I walked Buddy into the pet store at the front of the building. I bought him a leather collar and matching leash, a pinch collar, food and water dishes, organic kibble, and medicated shampoo. I also let him pick out his own toys and tennis balls. He selected a stuffed orange dragon that squeaked when you squeezed it, and a hedgehog that honked.

By the time we'd finished shopping it was 10:45. Once again I appealed to Karen, asking her to break policy by only fifteen minutes, and this time she relented. We all scampered out to the parking lot where Buddy watered a couple of bushes and then happily climbed into the back seat of the BMW.

We drove back to the marina and walked Buddy around the grounds. My original plan had been to leave the pup with Elizabeth, but now that I had him, I didn't want to leave him behind. I made a quick call to Sam, informing him that I'd be arriving with my new four-legged friend in tow. I warned him that Buddy might be a little shy at first. Sam grunted in response.

Buddy and I arrived at Sam's office a few minutes before noon. I knocked on the door and shortened Buddy's leash. Sam is a big man with a powerful presence, so I didn't know how Buddy might react to him.

"It's open," he called out.

I pushed open the door and let Buddy drag me inside. He pulled me into every corner of the front office before aiming his nose down the hall toward Sam's private domain.

Sam was seated in the visitor's chair in front of his desk when we entered. He had his hands on his knees, knuckles out, and he didn't move when Buddy entered the room.

"Hello, boy," he said softly.

Buddy stopped in his tracks and his hackles went up. He sniffed the air between himself and Sam, then lowered his head and leaned in, sniffing Sam's shoes. He wagged his tail one time and took a single step forward. He sniffed Sam's left hand, then his right, and wagged some more. Finally he turned around and sat down on Sam's feet.

Sam grinned and rubbed the top of Buddy's head.

"Hi, Sam," I said. "I didn't know you spoke doglish."

He chuckled, looking down at Buddy. "He's a good dog," he said.

Eventually Sam stood up, dislodging Buddy, who turned and licked his hand. Sam shuffled around behind his desk.

"So, Nicoli. What have you learned?"

I felt like the aspiring pupil I had once been.

"I have learned, Sensei, that Martin Wallace is a control freak, a voyeur, and an asshole. Have you eaten?"

"I grabbed a burger. Let's go talk to Boscalo's neighbors."

Gary Boscalo lived on Vanessa Drive in San Mateo. Sam and I took separate cars because I didn't want Buddy to shed all over Sam's interior and because I thought being in an unfamiliar car might make him insecure. Although he'd adapted to my little Bimmer pretty quickly.

Vanessa Drive is a middleclass residential neighborhood between Delaware Street and Highway 101. Sam got there before I did, but just barely. When I pulled up he was standing on the sidewalk across from Boscalo's house. I

parked the 2002, hooked Buddy's leash to his
collar, and walked over to Sam.

As I approached, he turned to face me.
"You're not planning on bringing the dog
along are you?"

"Yes, I am. I don't want to lock him up in
the car. He'll be good."

"I'm not disputing that, Nicoli. But some
people don't like dogs."

"I'm bringing him."

"Fine." Sam turned away from me and it
looked like his shoulders were shaking. Was he
laughing at me?

I followed him to the house directly across
the street from Boscalo's. As we approached
the front door we could hear the blare of a TV
coming from inside the house, blasting out
cartoons. I knocked on the door. A minute
passed and no one answered, so I rang the
bell. It was another minute before a woman
in her late twenties opened the door. She was
dressed in jeans and a tee-shirt. Behind her
were two toddlers of indeterminate gender,
both of whom immediately began squealing,
*"Gawgie!"* at the sight of Buddy.

I shortened the leash and the woman tried
to grab hold of her kids, but they were too
fast for her. In that instant I could foresee an
endless stream of lawsuits that would drain

my bank account for the rest of my life. Then Buddy began licking their grimy little faces and my fears vanished. The kids ran their hands over his head and back as Buddy washed any exposed flesh he could find.

"Can I help you?" the mother asked, keeping an eye on her kids.

I was caught up in the joy of children with a dog. I didn't want to spoil the moment by telling her why we were there, but I did anyway.

"My name is Nicoli Hunter and this is Sam Pettigrew. We're conducting an investigation."

She looked at me for a moment and then a light snapped on in her eyes. "Oh," she said. "Is this about Gary's wife and daughter? I heard about it from Janice." She nodded toward the house adjacent to Boscalo's. "Terrible," she murmured, shaking her head.

"May we come in?" I asked.

"Oh, I'm sorry. Of course."

She stepped back and allowed me to enter, towing Buddy and her two children. Sam brought up the rear.

"The house is a mess," she said apologetically. "The house is always a mess."

We all trooped into the living room and she lowered the volume on the TV. It's possible she was afraid she might have a riot on her hands if she turned it off completely.

I sat down on the couch and Sam settled into an armchair.

"I didn't catch your name," I said.

"Arleen Thomas."

She stood up briefly and shook my hand and then Sam's. Her hand was warm and dry, and her grip was firm.

"What were your names again?" she asked.

"I'm Nicoli Hunter," I said.

"Sam Pettigrew," said Sam, smiling benevolently at the harried young mother.

Arleen looked from one of us to the other and her gaze settled on me.

"We need to know anything you can tell us about Gary's relationships with his wife and daughter." I glanced down at the printout I'd brought along. "Jennifer and Melanie?"

That went over like a lead balloon. Arleen looked down at the coffee table, then she looked at the TV, and at her two toddlers who were still enthusiastically petting Buddy. "Kids, why don't you go to your room and see if you can find a toy for the nice doggy to play with."

Getting her kids out of earshot. This might be promising. When they were gone she said, "Is this going to get Gary in some kind of trouble? Because God knows that man has enough problems already."

"It's just background information," I said. "No one wants to get Gary in trouble."

She stared at me for a moment and then said, "He kind of has a temper. He was arrested for beating Jennifer up once. I used to worry about little Melanie. You know, kids can't defend themselves. But I never heard anything about him hitting Melanie."

I looked at Sam.

"Arleen," he began. "We'd like to ask you some more questions about Gary, but it's important that you keep this conversation to yourself. Can you promise to do that?"

"I'll have to tell my husband," she said. "I tell John everything."

"That would be fine," Sam said. "What we need to know is if you've noticed Gary going out in the middle of the night, or very early in the morning."

She turned to me as though I was going to give her the answer. "What's this really about?" she asked.

"We're researching the background of each passenger to determine their potential life insurance value."

She shook her head. "That's not a routine question," she said.

"No, but it's important."

She glanced at Sam, then back to me again.

Finally she said, "Once or twice, maybe. I just thought he was going for long drives because he couldn't sleep."

I felt an adrenaline rush. "Any chance you can remember the dates?"

"Oh, I don't know," she said. "I don't think so."

"How about the days of the week?"

"I'm not sure. I'll have to think about it."

The two kids stormed back into the room, each carrying a stuffed animal. The blond had a bunny and the brunette had a fuzzy yellow duck. They descended on Buddy, who was more than happy to chew on their toys, rolling onto his back and holding the bunny in his mouth and the duck between his paws. The toddlers giggled hysterically at his antics and I would have sworn he was smiling.

I couldn't think of anything else to ask, so I took out my wallet and handed Arleen one of my business cards. "Please call me if you remember any details," I said. "And please ask your husband not to discuss this with anyone, especially Gary."

When we were outside and Arleen's door was closed, we could hear the kids screaming for the gawgie to come back.

"You still think it might be a problem to

have the dog along on interviews?" I asked. I couldn't help it. Sam was so used to being right.

He looked at me sideways and said, "Humph."

# CHAPTER 17

WE KNOCKED ON FOUR MORE doors that afternoon, but no one else was home. I wasn't surprised. Considering the neighborhood, everyone was probably at work.

We drove back to Sam's office and I found a soup bowl in his kitchen, which I filled with water for Buddy. He drained the bowl quickly, so I refilled it before settling into a visitor's chair across from Sam. I checked my watch. It was only 1:45.

"I think I'll go check out the businesses around Wallace's office. Will you be in the office later today, so we can go over everything we've learned?"

"Hard to say. Give me a call."

I walked Buddy out to the parking lot and he jumped back into the 2002. I rolled the windows down far enough to provide the puppy with airflow and scents, but not enough to allow him to fit his head through the gap.

When we arrived in Belmont I parked down the street from Wallace's office and considered my options. There was a Thai restaurant across the street, a bank behind his office on a side street, and a pawnshop next door.

I hooked Buddy's leash to his collar, quickly skirted past Wallace's office, and approached the pawnshop. The sign on the door indicated that they were closed. I shaded my eyes and looked through the window. The lights were on inside and there was a tall, bearded man behind a counter in the back of the store. He was seated on a stool next to an open gun safe, and he appeared to be cleaning an assault rifle. I quickly stepped back from the door, but it was too late. He'd seen me.

The man approached the front of the store with a set of keys in his hand, unlocked the door and turned the sign around. He opened the door and peered out at me and Buddy.

"Can I help you?" he asked in heavily accented English.

He was about six-two and muscular without being bulky. His hair and beard were brown, turning to gray. His eyes were steel blue. I guessed he was in his late forties. He was dressed in jeans and a plaid flannel shirt. Buddy growled deep in his throat and I shortened the leash.

"I hope so," I began. "I'm interested in anything you can tell me about your neighbor." I tilted my head to the right, indicating Wallace's office.

The man stepped outside and looked at the law office as though he'd never seen it before. Then he stepped back inside and said, "Why don't you come in?"

"Okay to bring my dog?"

"Sure. I like dogs." Buddy was still growling softly. "I don't think he likes me, though."

"He's a little shy," I said. "My name is Nicoli Hunter." I extended my hand.

"Aleksei Sidorov," he said, and shook my hand firmly. "Oops," he said, wiping his hand on his jeans. "I think I got some gun oil on you. Let me get you a rag."

I smelled my hand and recognized the familiar scent of Hoppes. He handed me a rag and I wiped off most of the oil, but the scent would be with me all day. It reminded me of target practice with my dad. We'd always cleaned his rifle after firing it.

"Sidorov," I said, handing back the rag. "Is that Russian?"

"I'm from Siberia," he said. "Weather's better here. So why are you investigating Wallace?"

"Do you know him?" I asked.

"We don't socialize, but I know who he is. You a cop?" he asked, as he smoothly lowered the assault rifle below the display case.

"I'm a PI," I said, smiling, hoping to put him at ease. "My dad grew up in Irkutsk."

He raised an eyebrow. "Hunter? Doesn't sound Russian to me. You speak the language?"

"I know a couple of tongue twisters, but Dad didn't speak much Russian at home." I repeated the two tongue twisters my father had taught me when I was a kid and Aleksei laughed at my accent. I'm not good with foreign languages.

"Okay, Nicoli," he said. "What do you want to know?"

"I want to know if you've observed anything unusual in Wallace's behavior lately, and if you ever saw him with his wife and kids. And I don't want you to tell him I was asking."

Aleksei squinted at me from under his bushy brows, his eyes measuring me. I stared boldly back at him like I used to do with my dad. More often than not glaring at my father got me cuffed on the side of the head, but I knew it would earn me respect. After a minute Aleksei sat down on his stool.

"I've seen him with his wife a couple of times," he said. "I step outside to smoke, so the customers don't get offended. One time I was outside smoking and Wallace and his wife came out the front door of his office. I knew it was his wife because she was cowering. A mistress wouldn't cower. She had parked her car on the street and he was yelling at her for not parking in the lot. I don't like him much."

"What about the other time?" I asked.

He looked at me.

"You said you'd seen him with his wife a couple of times," I reminded him.

"You're kind of pushy," he said.

"Thank you."

"It wasn't a compliment."

"I guess that depends on your point of view."

He grinned at that, and his eyes sparkled without warmth. "The other time I was walking over to the restaurant," he said. "Business was slow, so I was going to get some lunch. I glanced in the window as I was walking by and I saw him down the hall, fucking his wife on the desk."

I let the image sink in before asking, "Are you kidding me?"

He shook his head.

"How did you know it was his wife?"

"Because of the angle of the desk. I could see her face."

"They were on the desk in the back office, but you could see them through the front window?"

"Look, you don't have to believe me, but that's what I saw."

"I'm asking because I was in his office the other day and I couldn't see a desk down that hallway."

"So maybe he moved the desk."

*Huh.* "Anything else unusual going on?"

He shook his head. I could tell I'd worn out my welcome, so I gave Aleksei my business card.

"If you think of anything else I'd appreciate a call."

He nodded, but I didn't imagine he'd be calling. I thought about Wallace having sex with his wife on the desk and wondered how that played into the voyeur personality type. Maybe someone who liked watching would also like being watched. Maybe he'd moved the desk specifically so that they could be seen from the street, and then moved it back again later. Interesting guy. Disgusting, but interesting.

I put Buddy in the car, leaving the windows cracked, and walked across the alley to the bank. I entered the lobby and scanned the interior. After a quick analysis of each employee seated at a desk I spotted the one I was looking for. She was in her late thirties and had an open box of Godiva chocolates in front of her. Brown hair professionally streaked with blonde, a little overweight, carefully applied make-up, pretty, but not beautiful, and no wedding ring. I approached the bank manager with a smile.

"Hi there," I said. "I wonder if you might have a few minutes to speak with me."

She smiled sweetly, pushed the box of Godivas forward, and said, "Have a seat. I'm Sharon Stamper."

I held out my hand and she shook it. Hers was warm and soft, and her grip was gentle.

"Nicoli Hunter," I said. "I'm a private investigator."

I watched her eyes widen with excitement.

"I'm conducting background investigations on the victims of a recent accident," I continued, "and I need your help."

Her mouth formed an O, and I knew I had her. "Of course," she said. "Anything I can do."

"You'll have to keep everything we discuss to yourself," I countered.

I knew that was going to be challenging for Sharon. Unless I missed my guess she was an enthusiastic gossip.

Her eyes skittered around the bank for a minute before she said, "No problem."

"Great. You have a neighbor on the other side of the alley." I pointed out the back window.

Sharon leaned forward in her chair, peering at Wallace's building. "Yes," she said. "I know Mr. Wallace."

"Have you ever seen him interacting with his wife or his children?"

Sharon looked out the window again, as if that would give her better access to her memories. Maybe it would. Some memories are visually triggered, some audibly, and others by a familiar scent.

She turned back to me. "He killed her didn't he?"

She'd phrased it like a question, but her tone was certain. She'd given this some thought.

"What makes you think that?" I asked. My purse was in my lap, so I slipped my hand inside and turned on the mini-recorder.

"The way he was always yelling at her and pushing her around. That man isn't happy unless he's making someone else miserable. He came in here when he first opened his office and said he was thinking about changing banks. I talked to him because Gretchen was busy helping someone else. He wanted unlimited transactions for free with no minimum balance in checking or savings. Can you believe that? We don't do that for *anybody*. But mister high-and-mighty seemed to think that because we were going to be neighbors he should have special privileges. I tried to be nice about it, but he just wouldn't take no for an answer. He was extremely rude." Her face flushed at the memory.

"How long ago was this?" I asked.

"About three years, I guess. I finally had to ask him to leave. I said I was sorry that I couldn't offer him what he wanted, and he glared at me with so much rage I was afraid he was going to hit me or something. I almost pressed the panic button. I have this button under my desk that causes Charlie's pager to vibrate." She pointed to the front of the bank where a uniformed security guard stood. He was at least eighty and wasn't a smidge over five feet tall. I didn't see a gun on Charlie's belt, but he probably had a taser or some pepper spray.

"Then what happened?"

"He took one of my chocolates and left. My heart didn't stop pounding for an hour."

"Scary guy, huh?"

"He really is."

"Has he come into the bank since that day?" I asked.

"I don't think so. At least not when I was working."

"Did you ever see him strike his wife?"

The information I was gathering would help with character profiling, but it wouldn't be worth anything in court. If Wallace was the killer we would need to find some physical evidence linking him to the ATC murders in order to get him arrested and convicted.

"Not strike her exactly," Sharon was saying. "But I saw him shove her a couple of times, and he always seemed to be yelling at her about something, poor woman."

"Thank you, Sharon." I gave her my card. "If you notice him doing anything that seems unusual, I'd really appreciate a call."

She promised she would call, and her eyes were bright with anticipation when I left.

I took a quick walk through the Thai restaurant before going back to my car. You couldn't see into Wallace's office from the restaurant windows, but nothing ventured and all that. I approached the teenager behind the counter, whose nametag read Rose, introduced myself, and asked her if she knew who Wallace was. She said she'd seen him coming and going, but that he'd never come into the restaurant when she was working. And, no, she hadn't noticed him interacting with his wife and kids.

I called Sam on my way back to the marina, putting the smartphone on speaker.

"What have you got for me, Nicoli?" he asked by way of greeting.

"Remember when we were in Wallace's office?"

"I do."

"Did you happen to notice the position of his desk?"

"You mean the reception desk?"

"No, I mean *his* desk. Did you look down the hall into his private office?"

"Yes. But I didn't see any desk. Why?"

"Because his neighbor, the pawnbroker, says he was walking by on his way to the Thai restaurant one day and saw Wallace having sex with his wife on the desk. He says he glanced in the front window and the desk in the back office was visible from the street. Also, a young woman who lives across the street from Wallace says he spies on her with his camera, using a telephoto lens. Three different people have witnessed him striking or shoving his wife on more than one occasion."

"Interesting," he said.

"I know none of this makes Wallace a killer," I went on, "but it does make him the kind of person who would seek revenge. He has a temper." I paused. "What did you find out about Fragoso?"

"There may be more to that man than meets the eye," he said. "At least I hope there is, because what meets the eye is pretty sad. His neighbors say he keeps to himself. Drinks more beer than is good for him. Generally gets a little friendly when he's drinking, however, rumor has it that when his wife was alive she would nag him about it and he'd get pretty angry. No reports of domestic violence, but he'd yell at her loud enough for the neighbors to hear.

"According to the apartment complex manager he pays his rent late three or four times a year, but he always pays. Only one neighbor actually knew his name. I kept having to describe him, or say the guy in 2B. That's what I meant by sad. No money, no friends, that I met anyway, and now his wife and eight-year-old daughter are dead.

"When I asked his neighbors if they'd heard him go out early in the morning or late at night, I got mixed responses. The guy across the hall said he's heard Fragoso's apartment door close in the middle of the night, but he never noticed the time. The old lady who lives next door says he's quiet as a mouse, but I think she's mostly deaf. The next door neighbor on the other side says he sometimes hears voices coming from Fragoso's apartment at night. He recently heard what sounded like an argument, which got pretty heated, but the only voice he heard was Fragoso's and he couldn't make out what was said. The guy could have been ranting alone in his apartment.

"The same neighbor said he once saw smoke coming from under Fragoso's door. He was going to call the fire department, but decided he'd knock on the door first and get Fragoso out. He knocked, but there was no answer, so he knocked louder, and after a minute Fragoso came to the door. The guy said he looked like a fucking zombie, his exact words. His eyes were unfocused, his mouth was hanging open, there was even a little drool dripping down his chin. The neighbor asked what was burning and Fragoso said, "Oh shit," and just walked away. Left the door open. So the neighbor went into the kitchen where he found an empty frying pan sitting on a lit burner. The range is electric, but the burner was on high so the pan was smoking like crazy. He turned off the stove and set the pan in the sink, then went looking for Fragoso. Found him in the living room, curled up asleep on the couch."

"Sleepwalking?" I asked.

"Probably."

"People who sleepwalk are usually dealing with a subconscious conflict. Could be he's tortured over the loss of his wife and daughter," I said. "You saw how emotional he was."

"Yeah. That's probably what it is. So what is your gut telling you, Nicoli?"

"I don't know if it's my gut, but I really like Wallace for this."

When I got back to the marina I took Buddy for a quick walk, then I grabbed the kibble and toys out of my trunk and loaded them into a dock cart. It was a juggling act, dealing with the cart and the puppy on a leash, but I managed.

We stopped by D'Artagnon's boat, and Kirk was home. He held open the aft gate so D'Artagnon could step onto the dock. I breathed a sigh of relief at the ease with which he was moving. He really was going to be fine. The two dogs touched noses, then did the traditional ID check with a lot of butt sniffing and tail wagging. It looked like the boys were going to be great friends.

Before Buddy and I continued down the dock to my Cheoy Lee I gave Kirk a quick hug and said, "I'm so glad he's okay. Thank you for calling to let me know."

Kirk nodded and turned away quickly.

As I lugged my bundle of puppy supplies onto the boat Buddy jumped from my dock steps onto the deck, but hesitated at the top of the companionway leading down into the galley. I backed down the steps and offered him a dog biscuit from my pocket. Problem solved. He put one paw on the top step, then leaped the rest of the way down, landing at my feet. He wolfed down the biscuit, licked my hand, and wagged happily.

I filled his new water and kibble dishes, and stifled a yawn, realizing I was exhausted. After he'd finished eating I pulled a spare blanket out of the hanging locker and got Buddy settled on the blanket next to the bed, then curled up on top of the bunk and sank into a contented sleep.

When I woke up someone was snoring softly on the pillow beside me. I flipped on a lamp and looked at the bedside clock. It was 6:11. I rolled over and found myself face to face with a big, wet nose. Buddy was curled up on the bunk next to me. I reached out to stroke his face and he woke with a start, scrambled backward, and slid off the edge of the bunk onto the floor.

"It's okay," I said, trying to calm him. "It's just me."

He looked a little embarrassed, but promptly jumped back up on the bed and licked my face. I ruffled his ears and got to my feet. "You want to go for a *walk*?"

His big brown eyes signaled recognition of that word. I grabbed his leash and an empty plastic grocery bag, and led him outside. We walked across the street to the wildlife refuge. I didn't want to go too far in the twilight since I'd forgotten to bring a flashlight, so at the one-mile marker we turned and walked back. When we arrived at the boat I heard TV sounds. Buddy leaped down the companionway into the galley and growled low in his throat.

Bill appeared in the main salon doorway and said, "What the ...?"

The words were barely out of his mouth when Buddy's hackles sprang up all the way from his neck to the base of his tail. He crouched, bared his teeth, and roared out a big-dog bark.

"It's okay, Buddy," I said, grabbing his collar. "Good boy. Good watch dog."

I held his collar with one hand, leaned over to Bill, and touched his arm with the other.

"Put your hand out for him to sniff, palm down below his muzzle, slowly."

Bill gave me a sideways glance and slowly lowered his hand. Buddy tentatively sniffed the back of Bill's hand, but his hackles remained up and his tail was between his legs.

"Okay, now slowly squat down," I said.

I squatted too so we were both at Buddy's eye level. His tail started wagging. Buddy sniffed Bill's breath tentatively and then gave his nose a lick of approval. Bill reached out to scratch behind his ears, and the pup turned around. I knew what was coming and I didn't say a word. Bill scratched Buddy's rump above his tail and Buddy backed up, knocking Bill on his ass, then sat down on his belly, forcing Bill onto his back on the floor. I grabbed my smartphone and snapped a couple of pictures while Bill laughed quietly, causing Buddy to bounce up and down as he wagged his tail in Bill's face.

When Buddy finally let Bill up I offered him a Guinness, and asked the obvious question. "Did I forget we had plans tonight?"

He took a long sip from the Stout bottle, then shook his head. "No plans. I got off work at a reasonable hour and was just hoping to catch you at home. Is that a problem?"

"No. Not a problem. Have you eaten? I was going to make a chicken salad."

"That sound great," he sighed. "I guess I should have called, instead of just coming over."

I gave him a smile, but said nothing. We

were both still feeling awkward. I *did* wish he had called instead of just dropping by. I had given him his own gate key only so I wouldn't have to walk a hundred and twenty-five yards every time he came for a visit. Not so he could let himself in when I wasn't around. If it happened again I'd have to establish some boundaries, but I decided not to press the point tonight.

# CHAPTER 18

T HE KILLER WAS AWAKENED BY *the sound of his daughter's SpongeBob Squarepants alarm clock. He dressed quickly, grabbed a Rockstar energy drink out of the fridge and began to prepare for his next mission. This one was more important than any of the others. Today he would execute the supervisor.*

*He went to the garage and carefully duct taped an explosive device to his daughter's skateboard. Last night he'd equipped the board with a remote control engine from a toy truck that had been one of her favorite playthings. He loved the poetic justice of using her toys to kill the individuals who were responsible for her death. It made him feel as though she was with him again. He believed she would approve of what he was doing and how he was doing it. Making things right. He'd used her rubber snake to kill*

195

*Mayes, and her miniature Swiss Army knife to puncture Flannery's gas line. Unfortunately, he hadn't been able to think of something as clever with the Jensen woman and was reduced to using her blunt-tipped scissors to loosen the air hose.*

*He practiced maneuvering the skateboard around the garage using the remote. It was more difficult to steer with the extra weight, but he kept working at it. After an hour he was confident in his ability to control it and he placed the skateboard on the front passenger seat of his Hummer, bracing it with rolled towels so it would be secure while he drove. He set two remote control units on the console between the seats, one to drive the skateboard, and one to trigger the bomb.*

*He drove to the airport and parked outside the gated employee lot in the same spot he'd used while making his plans, and waited.*

*At 4:17 a.m. Paul Marks exited the building. The killer pointed his index finger at him, pulling an imaginary trigger and making a popping sound. Unaware of this scrutiny, Marks got into his BMW Z4 and started his engine. The killer started his at the same time. They made a caravan of two as he followed Marks onto Highway 101, and then onto 380, eventually merging onto Highway 280. They drove south on the nearly deserted freeway into the hills above San Mateo.*

*Marks took the Highway 92 exit and pulled off 92 at Alameda de las Pulgas. There was a traffic light at the intersection of Alameda and 92, and when he rolled to a stop at the red light the killer pulled in close behind him. He put the Hummer into park, opened his door, and set the skateboard on the asphalt. If the light lasted another minute he wouldn't have to use the driving control at all. He could just back up to 92 and trigger the explosive charge. There were no other cars around. As he shifted the Hummer into reverse, the light changed.*

# CHAPTER 19

I GOT A FUNNY FEELING IN my stomach as I unlocked the office door on Friday morning. My office has been broken into on occasion, so I'm naturally paranoid. The lock had been engaged, but I could feel something in the air, like an electrical charge left behind by someone who didn't belong in my space. I left the door open behind me and removed the Glock from its holster under my lap drawer. Buddy didn't seem startled by the gun, so I assumed he'd never heard one fired. I dropped his leash and told him to stay. Naturally he followed me everywhere I went. I walked into the kitchenette, then checked the closet and finally the bathroom. All were devoid of intruders. When I was satisfied that Buddy and I were alone in the office, I closed and locked the door.

The voicemail light was blinking, but I turned on the computer before pressing the play button. The message was from Paul and his voice sounded more strained than ever.

"You were right, Nikki," he said without preamble. "Someone tried to blow me up this morning on my way home from work. I managed to get away, but I didn't get his license plate number. Sorry. I can't believe this is happening. I'm calling that bodyguard you recommended as soon as I hang up."

I listened to the message a second time before looking up Paul's home number on my smartphone. My hands were shaking as I hit the call icon. The phone rang twice and then was answered by a woman. It was a voice I recognized, and I relaxed as soon as I heard her whiskey tenor.

"Marks residence."

"Lieutenant Quinn," I said. "It's Nikki Hunter. Remember me?"

"Anderson's girlfriend, right?"

I cringed. There's something about being called a 'girlfriend' that rubs me the wrong way.

"Right," I said, between clenched teeth. "Is Paul okay?"

"He's fine. Thanks for the referral."

"What happened this morning?"

"Apparently someone followed him when

he left work. He stopped at a traffic light and the other guy pulled right up to his bumper, opened his driver's side door, and put something on the ground. Paul was watching in his rearview mirror. He'd noticed he was being followed. Anyway, the light changed and Paul took off like a bat out of hell.

"The guy followed him, but Paul managed to put some distance between them. He slowed at the next red light he came to and that's when he spotted a skateboard speeding down the street behind him. It was unnerving, considering what's been happening to his staff. When the skateboard was right behind him, Paul hit the gas and gunned it through the red light. As he was pulling away the fucking thing exploded. It was a big explosion too. I stopped to look at the crater on my way over here. He says it pushed his car hard enough for him to lose control. He almost hit the center island on Alameda. But he's fine, and I'm here now."

"*Jesus Christ,*" I said. "Can I talk to him?"

"He's sleeping. I made him take a pill."

"How late will you be with him tonight?"

"It's my weekend, so I'm here till Sunday. I told him he shouldn't go back to work until this thing is resolved, but he says he's not hiding out at home. I'll be going to work with him tonight."

"Thank you, Lieutenant. By the way, what's your first name?"

"Marcia," she said. "But everybody calls me Quinn."

"Okay, Quinn. When he wakes up tell him I called. He can call my cell if he feels like talking."

"What's the number?"

I gave her my cell number and made sure she had my home and office numbers as well. When we hung up my hands were still shaking, but it was just the adrenalin. I knew Paul was as safe as he could be, now that Quinn was with him.

I started a pot of coffee, then called Sam, who answered after two rings, sounding cranky. I didn't waste words.

"Someone tried to kill Paul Marks this morning on his way home from work. There was a car following him, and a bomb attached to a remote control skateboard. If Paul hadn't been paying attention he'd be toast."

"Was he injured?" Sam asked.

"No. Close call, though. He hired a bodyguard and she's going to the airport with him tonight."

"Did Paul see what kind of car was following him?"

I sat silently for a moment as the

importance of what Sam was asking struck me like a physical blow. "I don't know," I said. "I'll call you right back."

I redialed Paul's home number. Quinn picked up after one ring.

"Marks residence," she said.

"Hey, Quinn, it's Nicoli again. I need to speak with Paul. It's urgent. Can you wake him up for me, please?"

"Hang on," she said, and dropped the phone with a painful clunk.

A moment passed before the extension was picked up. "Nikki?" Paul sounded groggy.

"Hi, Paul. How are you holding up?"

"I've been better," he said. "I hope you find this guy soon."

"Me too," I said. "That's why I'm calling. I need to know what kind of car he was driving."

"Didn't Quinn tell you?"

"No."

"It was a Hummer. A black one. It looked new."

"Did you see any part of the license plate number?"

"Too dark."

"Okay, thanks," I said. "Get some rest. I'll talk to you soon."

I hung up before Paul could ask any

questions. There was no time. This was the lead we'd been hoping for.

I called Sam back. "New black Hummer," I said.

Hummers were relatively rare. It should be easy to trace any black ones sold in the Bay Area in the last six months.

"Only one problem," Sam interrupted my train of thought.

"What's that?"

"Each of our subjects probably received a substantial settlement from the airline, and maybe from individual life insurance policies as well."

"So?"

"So if you wanted a car that couldn't be traced back to you, what would you do?"

"I suppose I'd pay cash, but the car still has to be registered with the DMV. You can't register a car under an assumed name."

"Nicoli," he said, "this guy is killing people. Do you really think he's going to worry about the DMV coming after him for not registering his new Hummer?"

"I see your point," I said.

Sam thought for a moment. "We'll each take half the list of surviving family members, starting with our top three candidates, and we'll check out their garages."

"I'll start with Wallace and Fragoso," I said.

"Okay." I could tell he was trying to figure out why I'd opted not to go back to Boscalo's neighborhood.

"They already know you at Fragoso's apartment building," I said.

"Fine," said Sam.

"I don't want to subject Buddy to another assault by those kids," I added.

"Okay," he said, but I could tell he was stifling a laugh.

Buddy and I took off a few minutes later. Our first stop was Fragoso's apartment complex in San Carlos. There were no Hummers parked in the garage under his apartment building. Not really surprising, considering the average income of apartment dwellers in this section of San Carlos. I drove around the neighborhood in case the suspect vehicle was parked out in the open where no one would think to look for it. After about ten minutes I moved on.

I didn't want to risk going back to Wallace's home without making sure he was at his office, so I drove there first. I checked the parking lot behind the building, and did not see a Hummer. I parked in the Thai restaurant lot and walked Buddy across the street to the law office, flattening myself against the front of the building and peering in through the glass door to see if the overhead lights were on. I imagined what I must look like to passing motorists. *Crazed female stalker with dog.* The lights in the office were on, so we jogged back to my car and sped off to the Belmont Hills.

I parked on the street directly in front of Rebecca and David's house. If Wallace came home while I was snooping around his garage I was screwed anyway, so there was no point in hiding my car. I hooked Buddy to his leash and we skulked down Wallace's driveway to the two-car garage. Actually, I skulked, Buddy pranced.

There were no windows on the garage door, so we walked around to the side gate. Before attempting to unlatch the gate I looked for any wires that might indicate the presence of an alarm system. I didn't see anything, so I reached over the top and felt around for a latch. I couldn't find one and was considering climbing over the thing when I felt a light tap on my shoulder. I leaped straight up in the air, spun around, and slammed myself back against the gate.

"Sorry," said Rebecca. "I didn't mean to startle you. The latch is on the bottom."

While my heart pounded in my chest and I made an effort to catch my breath, Rebecca bent down, reached under the gate, and slid a bolt to the left, then pushed the gate open into the side yard. "Hi, puppy," she said, scratching under Buddy's chin.

He wagged his tail and grinned at her.

When I was calm enough to speak I said, "Thank you. You scared the shit out of me. I thought you were Wallace."

"Sorry," she said again, giving me a brilliant smile that suggested she wasn't sorry at all.

I scanned the neighborhood to see if anyone else was watching. Although there was no one on the sidewalk, I thought I saw a face quickly moving away from the window next door.

I led Buddy into the side yard and when I tried to close the gate behind us, Rebecca slipped through.

"You can't be here," I said.

"Why not?"

"Because it's illegal and dangerous, and I don't want to be responsible for anything happening to you."

"I am the only person who is responsible for me," she said, lifting her chin defiantly.

"Suit yourself."

I tiptoed to the garage window and peered into the dark interior. There was a silver SUV in the slot closest to the window. I couldn't see beyond it to the other side of the garage. Rebecca leaned over my shoulder, trying to see what I was looking at.

"Have you ever seen Wallace driving a Hummer?" I asked.

"No," she said. "Why? Did something happen?"

"I can't tell you. Just let me know if you see him driving a black Hummer, okay?" I realized I sounded angry. "I didn't mean to snap," I said. "I just can't get you involved."

"I'm already involved. I live across the street. I've started closing the drapes so he can't see in, but I can't do that forever. When are you going to install the camera?"

"I'll try to get over here on Monday."

We walked around the back of the garage, hoping to find another window, but there wasn't one. The opposite side of the garage was connected to the house. There might be a Hummer in there and I just couldn't see it. We slipped out the gate and when I glanced at the window next door again, Gina Cirone was looking out. She waved at us. Rebecca waved back, a big smile on her face.

"*Shit*," I muttered.

Gina dashed outside and met us at the end of Wallace's driveway.

"What are you doing?" she whispered, as if talking quietly would make us all invisible.

"Can we go inside?" I asked, herding them toward Gina's back door.

We gathered in the kitchen and I closed the door and the blinds facing Wallace's house. After a moment's consideration, I opened the blinds again. I wanted to know if he came home.

"Gina," I began, "You can't tell anyone about this."

Gina crossed herself, and then raised her right hand as though taking a Catholic pledge.

"You too, Rebecca," I said.

Rebecca just stared at me.

"Okay. Sit down, both of you. I'm going to tell you what's happening, but if you whisper one word of this to anyone, lives could be lost. Is that clear?"

They nodded solemnly and sat down. I had their attention. I just didn't know if they could be trusted.

"Someone has murdered three air traffic controllers and attempted to kill a fourth in the last two months. All of them worked the same shift at the same airport, and they were all on duty the morning Wallace's wife and children were killed."

Both women gasped and Gina clutched at her chest.

"Are you okay?" I asked.

"My God," she said. "I knew that man was evil." She crossed herself again. "He didn't even care about those children. They were just possessions to him."

"Don't jump to conclusions. I don't have any evidence that Wallace is the killer. He just seems like the type of person who would seek revenge."

They nodded again, but neither was making eye contact with me. I could see the wheels turning. They were picturing Wallace as a murderer.

"I need you to promise you'll keep quiet about this and I need to know if you see Wallace going out late at night or very early in the morning, or if you see him driving a black Hummer. That's all. Don't follow him and don't let him see you watching. Don't take any chances." They silently nodded again. "*Say* something."

Rebecca protectively put her hand on Gina's arm. "We'll keep quiet," she said. "And we'll keep an eye on Wallace, discreetly."

I gave Gina one of my business cards, writing my home and cell numbers on the back.

"I need to go," I said. "Call me if anything happens."

Rebecca stood up and threw her arms around me. "Thank you," she whispered.

I let her hug me for a moment before pulling away. I stepped back and looked her in the eye. "We don't know that it's him, Rebecca."

"No, but you suspect him."

I shook my head. "Are you going to be disappointed if someone else turns out to be the killer?"

"Probably. But for now, it's enough that I'm not the only one who thinks that man is twisted."

I left them at Gina's kitchen table, working out a schedule so that one of them would always be watching Wallace's house.

I drove back to the marina and gave Buddy a long drink from the hose in the driveway. Then I took him for a quick walk around the grounds. After our walk we went down to the boat where I selected a couple of large plastic bowls, filling one with kibble. We went up to the office where I set the kibble dish on the floor in the kitchenette. I filled the other bowl with water, and placed it next to the kibble.

Buddy looked up at me, took a few laps of water, sniffed at the kibble, and then ambled across the office and planted himself on the floor between my desk and the front door. He would be between me and any potential intruder, and he would also be in a position to stop me if I tried to leave the office without him. Clever boy.

I pulled the printout from my purse. I was excited about the Hummer lead, but I wasn't thrilled about the amount the time it would take to find out if any of the family members of the plane crash victims had purchased one in the last two months.

I was plotting the route from the office to the homes of three female surviving family members, each of whom had lost her husband and at least one child, when my phone rang. I picked it up without checking the display, lost in the bowels of MapQuest.

"Hunter Investigations."

"Nicoli, it's Sam." The static on the line told me Sam was calling on his cell phone.

"What's up?" I asked.

"I'm following the subject," he said, meaning Boscalo. "He just happened to be home when I dropped by, so I waited around. When he drove out I was able to see into the garage and what we're looking for isn't in there, so I thought I'd see where he was headed on a weekday afternoon. He went to a storage facility on Delaware Street. I took a chance and drove in behind him. I just hope I can get back out again."

"Is that why you called? You need me to break you out of a storage facility?"

"No, Nicoli. I called you because he's got a ten-by-thirty foot unit and I can't get close enough to see what's inside without alerting him."

"Wait a minute," I said. "That's big enough to store a car!"

"Bingo," Sam declared. "I need you to take a look at unit D-twenty-four tonight after they close. You think you can do that without getting yourself in trouble?"

"No, but I know someone who can."

I told Sam about the contents of Wallace and Fragoso's garages, and about the three female surviving family members I planned to check out next. Not that I expected anything to come of it. My gut told me we were on the right track with our original suspects, but Sam had taught me never to assume anything. So I was being thorough. He said he'd be checking on a woman who lived in the South Bay area, himself.

When Sam and I hung up I called Elizabeth. I was going to ask her boyfriend, Jack McGuire, the former cat burglar, to come out of retirement, and I needed her permission first.

"This is Elizabeth," she answered on the first ring.

"I need a huge favor."

"Hi, Nikki. How are you doing? More importantly, how is my sweet little Buddy doing?"

I looked down at the dozing canine. "He's adjusting nicely," I said.

"Excellent. So what can I do for you?"

"I need Jack to help me with a surveillance job tonight." You can't be too careful what you say on the phone, even on a landline.

"Surveillance, huh?"

"I wouldn't ask, but it's an emergency. My friend's life is in danger."

"Is this the investigation you told me about?"

"Yes. I didn't want to call Jack without talking to you first."

"Good thinking. I'd like to know the details. Can I drop by your office after work?"

"Of course."

"Okay. I'll be there around five."

"I'll see you then. Oh, and can you watch Buddy for a couple of hours tomorrow?"

"I'll take him all day if you want."

"No need. I'm just having lunch with my

213

high school friend Cher, and you know how busy The Pelican is on the weekend. Buddy's still a little skittish around strangers."

"I'll be at the marina all day tomorrow. You can drop him off on your way to lunch."

"Great. Thank you."

I called Bill next.

"Are you working late tonight?" I asked.

"Not that I know of. Why?"

"I have to go out and I was wondering if you could babysit Buddy onboard the boat. He hates it when I leave him in the car." I could leave him with Elizabeth, but she has a cat, and I wasn't sure Buddy would be safe around K.C., aka Killer Cat. He spends his days prowling around the marina, but his nights with Elizabeth.

"What time do you need to leave?" Bill asked.

"Seven-thirty."

"I can do that."

"Thanks. I'll see you later."

I was getting behind with my regular clients, but the urgency of Paul's case couldn't be ignored, so I finished plotting the route to my selected next of kin candidates, and Buddy and I hit the road again.

We made stops in San Mateo, San Bruno, and San Francisco, driving around residential neighborhoods in each case, searching for a black Hummer. Because San Francisco garages are so close to the street, I was able to discreetly peek in that one, but I wasn't as fortunate with the San Mateo and San Bruno neighborhoods. Too many people were home, as was evidenced by the number of cars parked on the streets and in driveways.

We were back at the office by 4:30. I checked in with Sam, letting him know the results, or lack of results, of my property search. He hadn't had any luck either. I told him I'd call in the morning with news about Boscalo's storage locker and ended the call.

Buddy and I walked out onto the lawn in front of the office to wait for Elizabeth. It was a sunny afternoon, and I felt guilty about keeping him indoors so much of the time. He watered a few shrubs and then rolled around on the grass with his feet up in the air. When he stopped rolling he stayed on his back, mouth open, exposing his beautiful white teeth. He was still like that when Elizabeth showed up.

"Ooohhh, look at the baby boy," she cooed.

Buddy rolled over and jumped to his feet in one smooth motion, then crouched like a cat, leaped into the air, and flung himself at Elizabeth. She caught the pup in her arms and tumbled backwards onto the lawn, her eyes wide.

"Wow," she said.

"I think he likes you."

Elizabeth giggled and scratched behind his ears, and he sat down on her belly.

"So, tell me," she said from her prone position on the lawn.

"I have to break into a public storage facility tonight, and then break into one of the lockers without getting caught and without leaving a trace. I need Jack."

"What are you looking for?"

"We know the killer drives a black Hummer. I need to see if there's one parked in the locker."

"Okay. But if you get caught and Jack gets in trouble, you have to fix it. He's finally an honest man and it would be too ironic if he got caught breaking and entering for a just cause."

"I promise I won't let anything happen to him." It was an empty promise and we both knew it, but sometimes you have to say the words anyway.

"I'll give him a call," she said. "Do you want to pick him up at his house?"

"That's what I had in mind."

"Do you need someone to watch Buddy tonight?"

ing over. I didn't think K.C.
ciate canine company."

ped Elizabeth to her feet and pulled
for a hug. Then she went through the
cked gate to the docks, and Buddy and I went
back into the office to shut everything down.

# CHAPTER 20

BILL ARRIVED AT 7:16 WITH a bag of Chinese takeout, filling the boat with the tantalizing aroma of deep-fried carbohydrates. He also had a binder under his arm.

I took the bag and set it on the galley counter, then glanced at the binder and said, "Homework?"

"I can't seem to get a fix on this one," he said.

"I have a little time. You want to tell me about it?"

I grabbed three egg rolls and a handful of pot stickers and tossed them on a paper plate.

Bill set the binder on the galley counter and slid it toward me. This was unprecedented behavior. Normally getting Bill to share information on an unsolved case is like pulling teeth.

I flipped the binder open and glanced at the crime scene photos. Caucasian male, face up on the ground. There appeared to be a single stab wound to his upper abdomen. Not a lot of blood. I looked at Bill.

"The victim was a registered sex offender," he said. "He was killed outside a daycare facility on Middlefield Road. No witnesses. None that we've located anyway. He was stabbed with a long, sharp blade. I can't help thinking this is too much of a coincidence. The guy was a pedophile, hanging out near a daycare center when somebody killed him. We may have a vigilante on our hands."

I paged through the reports, which included the victim's criminal history. He'd done time and been released, twice, for abducting and molesting children. I struggled with feelings of admiration for whoever had killed him. I have major issues with anyone who preys on the innocent.

"Who has access to the registered sex offender files?" I asked.

"Pretty much anyone who works in law enforcement. The files at the station are kept in a locked cabinet in investigations. Each file has the offender's record and registration form. The records department also has files on these guys, and those cabinets aren't locked."

"What about public access, and what about the families of the children he abducted?"

"There are two categories of sex offenders, those who are subject to disclosure and those who aren't. Sexually violent predators and sexually habitual offenders are subject to disclosure and are registered on the Department of Justice website. This guy was a habitual sex offender, so basically anyone with an internet connection could get his name, home address, and a list of his crimes. There are photos on the website too. The first thing we did was check the alibis of the affected families. One of them has moved out of state, and there's no record of any travel in the last month. The parents of the other child he was convicted of abducting were both at work at the time he was killed."

"Are you having trouble getting motivated?"

"Murder is murder, Nikki. No matter who the victim is."

"If you say so. I have to change clothes. Don't give Buddy too much people food."

I dressed in black stretchy jeans, a black long-sleeve tee shirt, and black running shoes, tucking my taser in my black leather jacket pocket.

I kissed Bill and leaned in for a hug. When I felt the tension melt out of my body

DINNER AND A MURDER

I let go, retrieved my purse, and jogged up the companionway. I glanced back over my shoulder and saw Buddy gazing up at me. "Stay," I said, holding up my hand like a stop sign before closing the hatch.

"What time will you be back?" Bill called out.

"I'm not sure, but it shouldn't be too late. Thanks for watching Buddy for me." I made my escape before he could ask why I was dressed like a ninja.

I was hoping the public storage facility wasn't one of those that has a manager living on the premises. If Jack and I got caught, I was afraid Elizabeth would never speak to me again.

As I pulled out of the parking lot I felt like part of me was missing. There was no warm puppy breath on the back of my neck. No one was licking my ear and pushing my head aside so he could stick his nose out my window. Buddy had only been with me for two days and already I missed him when he wasn't there. Maybe I'd have to rethink the idea of finding him a home with a fenced yard.

I wasn't picking Jack up until 9:30, and I wanted to see where Fragoso went after work, so I drove to Best Buy and parked near the entrance. I got out of the Bimmer and walked inside.

I hovered around kitchen appliances, peeking surreptitiously between the shelves into the home entertainment department until I caught a glimpse of him. Then I snuck back outside and circled the store on foot, looking for an employee entrance. I found a shipping and receiving dock, but I didn't think he was likely to exit that way, so I got back in my car and watched the front doors.

At 9:02 the last of the customers straggled out and one of the employees locked the doors from the inside. A few minutes later Fragoso came out, the same employee locking up behind him. I crouched down in my seat, even though the parking lot was fairly dark.

Fragoso stopped and lit a cigarette before walking to his car. He inhaled deeply and I remembered how good that used to feel. Then I remembered how hard it had been to quit. Not worth it.

I watched Fragoso walk to an old dilapidated VW van, about as far from a Hummer as you could get. He drove north on Highway 101 into Burlingame, and I followed. He took the Broadway exit and made the first right off of Broadway, then took an immediate left. He parked in front of a red brick duplex.

I doused my lights and pulled to the curb at the end of the street. Fragoso got out of his car, walked up the steps, and let himself in, turning the interior lights on as he stepped inside. The duplex had been dark before he entered, so he was probably alone in there. There was a garage, but he had parked on the street—maybe because there was a Hummer in the garage?

I made a note of the address and took off for Hillsborough.

I arrived at Jack's estate at 9:25. The gate was open so I pulled down the driveway and stopped in front of the main house. He was out the door before I shifted into park and didn't say a word as he got into my car.

"How are you, Jack?" I asked.

He gave me a stern look. Jack is normally pretty easygoing.

"You're mad at me, aren't you?"

He turned away and said, "Why would you think that, Nicoli?"

Oh man. I was in big trouble. He never called me Nicoli anymore, and his accent was more pronounced than usual.

"Because I went through Elizabeth to ask you for a favor, instead of coming directly to you?"

"And why should that make me angry?"

This was typical Irish banter. They always answer a question with another question.

"Because you're your own man and nobody makes your decisions for you?" I was beginning to enjoy this.

"So you think I might be upset with you because you asked Elizabeth for *permission* rather than asking me directly to help you with a little breaking and entering. Is that it now?"

"Your accent is showing," I said.

Jack was born here but raised by his grandparents in Ireland after his mom and dad were killed in a plane crash.

"Listen, Jack, Elizabeth is my best friend. I've known *you* for what, two months? It means a lot to Elizabeth that you've retired. If I had come to you and asked for help without talking to her first, *she* would have been pissed off at me. I hope this doesn't offend you, but I'd rather have you angry with me than Elizabeth."

He turned to look at me, a shadow of a smile on his face. "I suppose I can understand that."

I drove past the Delaware Avenue Public Storage facility so Jack could get a look at the layout. There was a small two-story building to the left of the gated entry. Lights were on in a loft apartment above the office. There was an onsite manager, and they were home. *Crap.*

I parked a block away and we walked around behind the lot. The storage facility, which took up half a city block, was surrounded by hurricane fencing, and there were two strands of barbed wire across the top of the fence.

"What have you got in the trunk?" Jack asked.

I thought about the question for a moment before I realized what he was asking. I jogged back to the car and dug a heavy beach towel out of the trunk.

When I got back to where Jack had been standing he was perched halfway up the fence with his left hand and the toe of his left shoe holding him in place. He looked like he was levitating there. He was dressed all in black, including a pair of black leather gloves. A black watch cap covered his red hair. In the few minutes I'd been gone he'd applied black greasepaint to his face. I wished I could snap a picture, but Jack wouldn't have the patience for that.

I handed him the towel and he draped it over the barbed wire, folding it in half for extra padding. He reached his hand down for me. I hoisted myself up onto the fence and Jack helped me over the portion of barbed wire covered by the towel. He waited until I'd dropped to the ground on the other side, and then flipped himself up and over the towel like a gymnast. He flicked the towel down from the barbed wire and tucked it under a bush, then took me by the arm and pulled me behind the trunk of a eucalyptus tree. He took something out of his fanny pack and handed it to me. It was a tube of black greasepaint.

"Do I have to?" I whispered.

"Do you want to get caught?"

I unscrewed the top of the tube and rubbed the noxious gunk all over my face, neck and hands. Then I wiped my greasy palms on my jeans. Paul would have to pay for the jeans. This stuff wouldn't wash out.

Jack took a small flashlight out of his fanny pack and whispered, "What's the locker number?"

"D-twenty-four."

He moved toward the nearest row of lockers and shined a narrow beam of light onto the area above the door. F-103. He moved the light one locker to the right and began silently walking toward the back of the facility. I followed. Halfway across the complex I turned to look over my shoulder, and when I turned back Jack was gone. He'd just vanished. This happens more often than you would think with Jack. I'm convinced he's half leprechaun.

There were no lights anywhere nearby, and I couldn't see two feet in front of my face.

"Jack," I hissed.

An arm snaked out of the dark, grabbed me by the wrist, and pulled me into the shadows. I sucked in a breath, but stopped myself before any sound could escape my lips.

"Relax," Jack whispered. "I thought I heard something, so I stepped into this alcove. I assumed you were right behind me."

As my eyes adjusted I realized we were in a long, narrow hallway off of which were doors to some of the smaller storage lockers. Jack and I stood perfectly still, pressed flat against the cold aluminum wall. I didn't hear anything, but I suspected he had extra sensory hearing from the years he'd spent as a cat burglar. I stared out into the yard, which now appeared lighter than the interior of the hallway. Jack kept his hand on my wrist, making sure I didn't move before he was certain it was safe. I felt protected and also a little irritated that he didn't trust me not to do something stupid.

After a minute, which lasted at least an hour, I heard a faint rhythmic clicking. I knew the sound instantly. There was a dog outside. Probably a Doberman or a Rottweiler, something ferocious and deadly. We were finished. We'd both be maimed and end up in jail, and Elizabeth would never speak to me again. I couldn't let that happen. I love dogs more than any other animal, but this wasn't just any dog. This was the end of my career, and Jack's future with Elizabeth would forever be tainted because of me. I reached into my pocket and pulled out my stun gun.

I felt Jack tense as the clicking grew closer. At the last possible moment I twisted my wrist out of Jack's grasp, nudged him behind me, and dropped to one knee, taser extended, ready to knock out the poor animal who was just doing its job. I was overwhelmed with guilt. My finger was poised over the switch and my heart was racing. I heard a sniffing sound. The creature had caught our scent.

Out of the darkness stepped a fluffy golden Cocker Spaniel. Big round eyes turned in my direction, and the pup's tail wagged tentatively. I caught myself before I pressed the switch, and had to stifle a laugh. How ridiculous was this?

I knelt in the doorway and whispered, "Hi, little fella."

The Cocker sniffed the air around me and then looked up at Jack. He growled softly.

"Sit down, right now!" I hissed.

Both Jack and the dog sat.

"Good boy," I whispered.

I reached out my hand, palm down, and the Cocker sniffed and then licked it, greasepaint and all. Dogs can always tell how you feel about them. I dug in my pockets until I found a dog biscuit, broke off a small piece, and held it out. He sniffed the offering and gently removed it from my hand. He chewed slowly, wagging the whole time.

I heard a shuffling noise and a woman's voice called out, "Sydney? Where are you, boy?"

The Cocker jumped up and ran in the direction of the voice. Jack and I stood slowly, not making a sound. I kept the stun gun out in case Sydney's mom decided to pay us a visit. We didn't move a muscle for several minutes and my legs started to ache from the tension.

Finally, Jack poked his head out the door and looked in both directions. "Stay here," he whispered.

"I'm coming with you."

He grimaced, but said nothing. Together we exited the hallway, moving slowly toward the back of the lot. Jack didn't want to risk using his flashlight again, so we had to get up close to the lockers in order to read the letters and numbers identifying them.

Eventually we found D-24. It was in the south corner of the lot and it was the largest locker on the premises with a garage-size overhead door. Jack held the padlock in his hand for a moment, studying it, before he opened his fanny pack and selected the appropriate picks.

I turned my back to him, watching for Sydney and anyone he might have with him. When I heard a soft *snick* I turned and saw that Jack had opened the padlock and was removing it from the overhead door. He placed it on the ground and then very slowly began raising the door. This was an agonizing process. Even when opened an inch at a time the door still made a ratcheting sound.

When the bottom of the door was two feet from the ground, Jack slipped underneath it and into the locker. I stayed outside for a full minute. When I felt confident that no one had heard anything, I rolled under the door and joined him.

"We don't have much time," he said.

There was a vehicle in the locker under a canvas car-cover, but it was too small to be a Hummer. Jack held his flashlight on the canvas and lifted a front corner. It was a red and white vintage Corvette.

"*Shit*," I hissed.

I turned on my own flashlight and started looking around the locker, hoping to find some other clue that would either vindicate or incriminate Boscalo. There was nothing.

"We have to go," Jack whispered. "If she heard the door opening she may have called the police by now."

That got my attention. We both slipped back under the door. Jack closed it as quietly as possible and replaced the padlock. We sprinted to the fence where we'd stowed my towel. Jack flipped it onto the barbed wire and adrenaline carried me up and over. Once safely outside I turned to watch as he vaulted himself up, clinging to the fence long enough to pluck the towel off the wire before dropping gracefully to the ground. An Irish Baryshnikov.

We bolted to the street where my Bimmer was parked. In the car, Jack removed his watch cap and quickly used it to wipe most of the greasepaint from his face. I used the towel, feeling the terrycloth stick to my skin. I started the car and drove away at the speed limit. As we turned from Delaware onto Concar we saw a police cruiser silently speeding south, its lights flashing.

"How much are you going to tell Elizabeth?" I asked.

Jack was quiet for a moment. I assumed he was thinking about the question.

"I'll have to tell her everything," he finally

said. "She's smarter than I am. If I leave something out she'll know, and then she'll never trust me again. I can't afford to have that happen, since I plan to spend the rest of my life with the woman."

I felt the breath catch in my throat. Was he saying what I thought he was saying?

"Have you picked out the ring?" I asked.

"It's being sized. Her hands are small."

I felt heat behind my eyes and bit my lower lip, trying to keep the emotion in check. Jack turned to look at me.

"What's wrong?" he asked.

*Men.* "Nothing," I croaked.

"Do you want me to drive?"

I blinked a couple of times and took a deep breath. "I'm fine, you idiot. I'm just happy for you, and for Elizabeth."

Even though I don't believe there will be a 'happily ever after' for me, I still get emotional about anything that resembles a declaration of love between other people. I always cry at weddings. I know, I'm a dichotomy—tough yet sensitive.

We made the drive to Hillsborough without saying another word. Jack used a remote to open the gate, and I parked in front of his house. We sat in the car for a few silent moments before I cleared my throat and said, "Thank you, Jack."

"My pleasure. You can call me any time. I like to keep my hand in."

I drove back to the marina thinking about relationships and commitment.

When I arrived home, Bill was on the settee in the main salon with Buddy draped across his lap, his hand resting on the dog's head. I kissed Bill on the lips and Buddy on the nose.

Bill examined the remaining grease paint at my hairline and on my hands, and a smirk formed on his handsome face. "Do I want to know?" he asked.

"Nope," I said. "I need a shower. Join me?"

# CHAPTER 21

T IMING WAS EVERYTHING, THE KILLER *told
himself. He shouldn't have rushed the
skateboard operation, but it was better this way.
He was glad the attempt with the bomb had
failed, because today would be the perfect day. It
wasn't about the sequence of events. It was about
the right date for the right mission.*

*He took out a steel bastard file and began
sharpening the broadhead tip of an arrow.*

# CHAPTER 22

ON SATURDAY MORNING BILL WAS up before dawn and went to the station to work on his sex offender homicide, saying he'd be back in a couple of hours if that was okay with me. It was.

After he left I called Paul at home.

"Marks residence," Quinn answered.

"You sound tired," I said.

"I wouldn't sound tired if people didn't call and wake me up."

"Sleeping on the job, eh?"

"Fuck you, Hunter. I can't be awake twenty-four hours a day. What do you want?"

"I want to know if Paul's okay and if anything suspicious happened last night or this morning."

"He's fine. We haven't seen the Hummer again. That doesn't mean the subject isn't out there watching. Probably driving a different car now, since he's been spotted."

"Please tell Paul that I called, and I'd like to hear his voice. Have they increased security at the airport?"

"They have a couple of guards stationed in the employee parking lot, and one at each building entrance."

"Better than nothing," I said. "Thanks, Quinn. I'll talk to you later."

She humphed and hung up the phone.

I walked Buddy down to the point where the marina parking lot meets the water, and we watched the sunrise. It was a cool, clear morning.

After our walk we unlocked the office and I called Sam to tell him what Jack and I had found in Boscalo's locker. He was understandably disappointed.

Then I pulled out the background reports on our three subjects. The first time I'd gone over them I had focused on any criminal activity. I needed to take a closer look. Maybe I was missing something.

I started with Wallace's background, reading every word this time. When I'd finished I opened my computer file on Paul's case and looked up the dates the three controllers had been killed. James Flannery had been blown-up on September 19th, Shirley Jensen had drowned on September 24th, Gordon Mayes had driven his SUV off an overpass on October 9th, and someone had attempted to kill Paul yesterday, on October 16th. None of these dates matched any significant dates in Wallace's background.

"Damn," I said. Buddy looked up at me, his ears pinned back. "Sorry," I said.

I used the bathroom, refilled my coffee mug, and sat down with Boscalo's background report. By 11:30 I knew everything there was to know about Wallace and Boscalo, and I was getting a headache.

I walked Buddy around the marina grounds and then down to the boat. Bill was back, sitting in the pilothouse playing his acoustic guitar. Buddy leaped from the dock steps onto the deck and pranced into the pilothouse where he planted himself on Bill's feet. Laughing, Bill set his guitar aside and ruffled the pup's ears as he looked up at me.

"You look tired, babe," he said.

"I didn't sleep well last night and I just read two lengthy background reports."

"Find anything?"

"Not yet. I think I'll take a power nap before my lunch with Cher."

I stumbled down the companionway, went

into the stateroom and stripped off my shirt and jeans. When I turned around both males were standing in the doorway watching me.

"What?" I said, climbing into bed.

"You want some company?" Bill asked.

"Okay," I said, "but make it fast, I really need a nap."

"You're such a romantic," Bill said, smiling.

At 12:30 I hopped into the shower feeling totally revived.

I fluffed up my curls and dressed in jeans and a quarter-zip sweatshirt. I pulled on my leather jacket, and walked Buddy over to Elizabeth's boat before going up to the restaurant. Bill had offered to stay with him, but I wanted Buddy to get used to Elizabeth too. He needed to understand that he had an extended family.

When we arrived at Elizabeth's trawler the door was open and the TV was tuned to one of those entertainment magazine shows. Elizabeth likes to keep track of what the stars are doing. I led Buddy up her dock steps and knocked. Elizabeth was at the sink with her back to us. When she turned around she was holding a jumbo-size doggie dish full of water.

"Hi, honey!" she exclaimed.

"Did you go shopping just for Buddy?"

"I did, and I had a wonderful time."

I looked around the boat, searching for K.C., but didn't see him anywhere.

"He went for a walk after breakfast," she said. "He's always home in time for dinner though."

"I don't know how Buddy is with cats yet."

"He'll be fine," Elizabeth said. She set down the dish and gave Buddy a hug. "Won't you sweetums?"

"Okay. I'll be back in a couple of hours."

"Take your time," Elizabeth said.

I stepped outside wondering if Buddy would try to come with me. As I walked up the ramp I turned and saw him standing in the doorway. Elizabeth was holding onto his leash. His brow was furrowed, but he was wagging his tail. Elizabeth said something to him and he looked up at her as I stepped through the gate. Maybe I was the one with separation anxiety.

# CHAPTER 23

I HAD FIVE MINUTES BEFORE I was due at The Diving Pelican so I stopped by the office. I still needed to read through Fragoso's background, and the tension had quadrupled since the attempt on Paul's life yesterday. The document was fifteen pages long so I stapled the pages together, grabbed a highlighter pen, and stuffed everything into my purse.

As I locked the office I glanced over at Elizabeth's trawler. The door was closed. I wondered if she and Buddy had gone for a walk, or if she'd had to close the door to keep him from following me.

Cher was seated at an outside table when I arrived at The Pelican.

"We have to order inside," I said, giving her a hug.

We tilted our chairs against the table to reserve it.

A few years ago when the restaurant which formerly occupied this space went belly-up, Bennett Zepeda, who is another boat dweller, quit his job and opened The Diving Pelican. It's not extremely well known outside of the boating community, but it should be.

Cher scrutinized the chalkboard menu listing the day's specials and selected a salad of fresh greens, Gouda cheese, walnuts, and mango. I ordered the meatloaf. I needed comfort food. We carried our beverages out to the table and sat facing the water.

"That's my boat," I said, pointing out the *Turning Point*.

Cher looked at the boat and smiled. "You were always so adventurous."

"I don't remember you backing away from any challenges."

"That's because I was with you. You made me feel like anything was possible."

"What are you talking about? We were teenagers, cutting class, sneaking smokes, and rolling up our skirts. How could I make you feel like anything was possible?"

"I don't know, but you did. I'm always afraid, Nikki. I didn't identify the feeling until

I started therapy, but it's been there for as long as I can remember."

I looked at her, digesting this information.

"I'm sorry," I said. "I didn't know."

"I think that's why I married Hal," she went on. "He's a big, strong man, and he made me feel safe when we first met."

"What about now?" I asked, feeling slightly awkward about prying into the personal life of a woman I hadn't spent time with in almost twenty years.

"Now I think I want a divorce," she said. "But I'm afraid to be alone."

"What are you afraid will happen?" I asked.

"That's a good question. My shrink asked me that."

"And what did you tell him ... her?"

"Her. Amber Tofford. She's wonderful. I told her that I was afraid of being lonely, and afraid I wouldn't be able to support myself. I never have, you know."

"How long have you and Hal been married?"

"Since college."

"That's a long time. If you divorce him won't you retain some of the assets the two of you have accumulated? I'm guessing, based on the size of that rock on your left hand, that half your joint assets would set you up for the rest of your life, providing you're frugal."

Our lunch was served and Cher placed a napkin on her lap, looking pensive. She took a bite of her salad and rolled her eyes. "This is incredible."

"Everything here is good. You didn't sign a pre-nup did you?" I asked, bringing her back to point.

Her mouth was full, but she shook her head.

"How much money do you have in checking, savings, stock, and property? How well off are you?"

"Why are you asking me these things?"

"I'm trying to identify whether or not you have a valid reason to be afraid."

"Oh," she said. "I guess on paper we're worth about four million."

"Okay, so after you pay the attorneys you'll have at least a million-five each, which you can convert into liquid assets if necessary."

"I guess. I haven't really thought it through. I haven't wanted to, but talking to you about this is making it real for me. Maybe that's good."

"It is." I squeezed her hand and offered an encouraging smile. "Okay, so you don't need to worry about money, and your fear of being alone is something you can work on with your therapist. You might learn to enjoy the independence, but if you *want* another relationship I'm sure you won't have any trouble finding a flock of willing suitors."

"If I divorce Hal for irreconcilable differences, will I still get half the money?"

"I think so. California is a community property state. Do you know any good divorce lawyers? Any friends recently divorced?"

"No."

"I've been divorced three times, but I handled each of them myself. I'll call my cousin Aaron and ask him for a referral."

"I thought you hated your cousin."

"Not so much anymore. Besides I don't have to like him to get you a referral."

My cousin Aaron was an asshole when we were kids. Now he's a criminal defense attorney. Go figure.

We ate our lunch and talked about what had been going on in our lives since high school. I told Cher the details of my three divorces. Her eyes widened when I told her my second marriage had been to a friend who wanted to immigrate. She was appropriately sympathetic when I told her that my most recent marriage had ended because I hadn't wanted children, and she laughed when I told her that Drew, my ex, now had triplets.

"Serves him right," she said.

"Do you have any kids?" I asked.

"Oh, no," she looked wistful. "I was afraid I wouldn't be a good mother. Because I'm so screwed up, you know?"

"As far as I can tell, you've only improved with age," I said. "The fact that you've stayed married to a man you don't love is a choice I might not have made, but it doesn't mean you're screwed up."

Cher put down her fork and reached for my hand. "You always say the right thing. Thank you for having lunch with me."

"Honey, I *wanted* to have lunch with you. I didn't realize how much I'd missed you until I saw you again." I squeezed her hand and saw tears form in her eyes. She asked me where the ladies' room was and excused herself.

I'd lost my appetite. I sat there wondering what had occurred in Cher's childhood that made her feel like she had no choices. Then I remembered Fragoso's background report was in my purse. I pulled out the sheaf of paper and scanned the first three pages, which were the criminal background I'd already read, then I turned to page four and read the significant dates.

Fragoso's wife, Mindy, had been born on October 9th and his daughter, Samantha, had been born on September 19th. *Holy shit!*

Those were two of the dates when air traffic controllers had been killed. I was sure of it.

The date of death for Fragoso's wife and daughter was mentioned in the report—August 16th. Someone had tried to kill Paul yesterday, on October 16th, exactly two months after the plane crash. I kept reading and saw that Chuck and Mindy had been married ten years ago on October 17th. *Today* was October 17th.

"Oh my God!" I said aloud, and a dozen heads swiveled in my direction. I stuffed the report back into my purse and ran for the ladies' room. Cher was coming out the door as I approached.

"I have to go," I said hastily.

"Is something wrong?"

"It's this case I'm working on. I just figured it out. I'll call you later and explain. I'm sorry to rush off."

I kissed her on the cheek and sprinted across the complex, reaching for my cell phone as I ran. I called Sam, slowing down long enough to select the right number.

"Pettigrew," he answered on the first ring.

"It's Fragoso!" I shouted into the phone.

"Nicoli? Are you all right?"

"I took a closer look at the background report on Fragoso. The dates match." I was unlocking my office door and breathing hard.

"I have to double check the file, but listen to this. Today is his wedding anniversary! He's going to kill someone today. Hang on."

I was at my desk. Grateful I'd left the computer on, I quickly opened the report I'd typed after having lunch with Paul. Gordon Mayes – October 9th. James Flannery – September 19th. Shirley Jensen – September 24th, I didn't have a match for that date in the background report, but I was sure it would be something significant to Fragoso. Maybe a first date with his wife, or the date he'd proposed. I was certain Paul's name would end up next to October 17th if I didn't do something fast.

"Nicoli? Are you still there?"

"Yes. I have to warn Paul."

"Take a breath. There's no point calling the police because they won't do anything until a crime has been committed. We're going to have to keep track of Fragoso ourselves. I'll call Best Buy to see if he's working today. If he isn't, I'll call his apartment manager and ask him to check his apartment and the garage. You call Paul and his bodyguard and fill them in, then call me back on my cell."

"Yeah, okay. Thanks, Sam."

I frantically dialed Paul's home number.

"Marks residence."

"Quinn, it's Nikki. The killer is Chuck

Fragoso. Mid-thirties, six-one, dark brown hair, mustache and goatee. Lost his family in a plane crash in August. Two of the controllers were killed on his wife and daughter's birthdays. Yesterday was the two-month anniversary of the crash that killed them, and today is their wedding anniversary. Can I talk to Paul?"

"Hang on."

Quinn put the phone down and I heard her call out. When I didn't hear a response from Paul the adrenaline pumping through my system kicked up a notch. Almost a minute passed before she came back on the line.

"He's not here. He was in the kitchen making sandwiches. I went to take a leak and when I came out the phone was ringing."

She sounded perfectly calm, but I knew the apprehension she was feeling.

"Look outside," I said. "Find out if the neighbors saw anything. I'm going to read the rest of this background report and then I'll call you back."

"Sounds good."

We ended the call and I quickly read about Fragoso's childhood. He'd been raised in South San Francisco, like me. Lower-middle-class family. Good grades in school. A couple of trips to juvenile hall for smoking pot when he was a teenager. His daughter had gone to

McKinley Elementary in Burlingame. I looked up the address online and printed the page. Mindy and Samantha were buried at the Skyline Memorial Cemetery. Maybe he'd want to kill Paul where they could watch. I made a note and kept reading. Mindy and Chuck had been married in Central Park, in San Mateo, at 2:00 p.m., on October 17th. It's amazing the detail you can get in background reports. I looked at my watch. It was 1:35. There was a rose garden in the park, with a gazebo. Lots of couples got married there. My gut told me that was where I'd find them. I dialed Sam's cell.

"Pettigrew."

"Paul's gone. Fragoso took him while Quinn was in the bathroom. There are three possibilities," I said. "I assume Fragoso's not at home or at work?"

"Correct."

"Okay. His kid went to McKinley Elementary in Burlingame." I read him the address. "You go there and search the school. Their graves are at Skyline Memorial. I'll send Quinn there."

"What are you going to do?"

"They were married at Central Park in San Mateo at 2:00 pm, which is too close for comfort. I'm going there, to the rose garden."

"Call me when you get there."

"Sure."

We hung up and I took the Glock out of my purse holster, checking to make sure the magazine was fully loaded. Then I grabbed an extra magazine from the gun drawer, locked the office, and ran to the parking lot.

When I was on the road I called Quinn back and told her about the cemetery. I also told her that Sam was going to the school and I was going to the park.

"You think they'll be at the park, don't you?"

"I don't know. They might be at the cemetery."

"You think they're at the park."

"Just go to the cemetery, Quinn. And be careful!"

"I'll go to the cemetery. But if you get yourself killed I'll tell everybody you were a fucking cowboy."

"*Fine!*"

I disconnected and drove at the speed of light toward San Mateo. It's about thirteen miles from the marina. I cranked the Bimmer up to 110 and hoped like hell there weren't any Highway Patrol officers on the freeway.

I pulled off 101 at 3rd Avenue West and slowed enough to stay alive on the city streets. At the first red light I checked my watch. It was 1:45. I could almost hear the clock ticking down the minutes Paul had left to live.

When the light turned green I floored the 2002, weaving around other motorists, eliciting angry honks and gestures. I arrived at Fifth and Laurel and turned left, pulled into a no-parking zone, and slammed out of the car with only my keys and the Glock stowed in my jacket pockets.

I ran full out toward the rose garden. There was a Japanese family taking pictures of each other in the gazebo. I slowed to a walk, not wanting Fragoso to notice me if he was in the area. When I reached the gazebo I stopped and scanned the surrounding area, turning in a slow circle, taking everything in. There were tourists and locals walking the paths. That was good for me—they offered cover—but dangerous for them.

As I pivoted to my left I spotted Paul and my heart stopped. He was seated at the base of an oak tree about ten yards away from me. His face was ashen and Fragoso was standing next to him, one hand behind his back and the other on Paul's shoulder. I grasped the situation instantly. Fragoso had threatened to kill innocent bystanders if Paul didn't cooperate. I knew Paul would willingly give his life to save a total stranger. That's the kind of guy he is.

Fragoso was probably waiting until the gazebo was unoccupied so he could kill Paul at the exact location where he and Mindy had been married. The fact that he was doing this in a public place meant Fragoso no longer cared about getting caught, which made him infinitely more dangerous.

I moved around the back of the gazebo, trying to stay hidden. There was a waist-high hedge growing in a maze-like pattern through the rose garden. I dropped to my knees behind it and crawled toward the oak tree. When I got to the end of the hedge I peeked out and noticed a child's archery set on the lawn next to Paul. The bow couldn't have been more than thirty-six inches long. Both the bow and the quiver looked like they were made of sturdy plastic, but I was willing to bet the arrows were steel-tipped. The skateboard chasing Paul's car and the rubber snake found in the remains of Gordon Mayes' SUV made sense to me now. Fragoso had been using his daughter's toys to kill the people he judged as responsible for her death. She must have been a tomboy.

I took a deep breath, pulled the Glock from my pocket, and stood. I leveled the gun at Fragoso and shouted, "*Police, freeze!*"

I hoped he wouldn't recognize me from our interview at Best Buy.

The crowd scattered at the sight of the gun as Fragoso slowly turned to face me. His expression remained neutral, and I was terrified that he would kill Paul regardless of the threat to himself.

*"Hands where I can see them!"* I shouted. *"Now!"*

Fragoso just stood there. I started moving toward him.

"Charles Fragoso, you are under arrest for the murders of Gordon Mayes, James Flannery, and Shirley Jensen. You have the right to remain silent. If you give up that right, anything you say can and will be used against you in a court of law. You have the right to an attorney. If you cannot afford an attorney one will be provided for you."

I was telling him his rights, hoping it would reinforce my character as a make-believe cop and convince him it was over and he might as well give up. It didn't work. Fragoso pulled a large-frame revolver from behind his back and pressed the muzzle against Paul's head.

*"Drop the gun!"* I shouted, but before the words were even out of my mouth Fragoso's head exploded and he slammed back against the oak. I automatically dropped to the ground,

flattening myself in the dirt. I turned my head and saw a solid-looking woman with short blonde hair, feet spread in a shooting stance, gripping a matte-black Desert Eagle double-handed. Her face was frozen in a grimace. Standing behind her was Sam Pettigrew, also aiming his weapon at Fragoso.

I rose slowly, putting the Glock back in my jacket pocket. I looked over at Paul, who was now on his hands and knees, throwing up on the lawn.

"Quinn?" I said softly. I had never met the Lieutenant, but I'd recognized her instantly. She looked just like she sounded—tough and rangy.

"Are you okay?" I asked. She flinched. "I think he's dead," I said, knowing the sarcasm would get through to her.

She lowered the gun, holstered it, and turned to look at me. Her face was almost as white as Paul's.

"Thanks," I said.

"You're an idiot," she said. "Nobody freezes when you say 'Police, freeze!'"

"You ever fire your weapon in the line of duty before?"

"Nope."

"Well, now you have."

"Yep."

Quinn secured the crime scene and dealt with the police, who were arriving in droves. Sam and I helped Paul onto a park bench. He was shaking uncontrollably, taking in great heaving breaths. His skin was clammy and his head and shoulders were covered with Fragoso's blood, bone, and tissue. I sat next to him, putting my arm around him, trying to avoid the gray matter.

"Try to breathe slowly," I told him, while gently pushing his head down between his knees. "You don't want to hyperventilate. Everything's okay now. You're safe, Paul. You're okay."

Of course he wasn't okay and he wouldn't be for a long time. He'd almost been killed and he was wearing the remains of his would-be assassin. He was in shock, severely traumatized, and would need extensive therapy. When he was ready to talk about it, I'd send him to Loretta. Besides being my personal shrink, she's the psychologist the RCPD uses for post-traumatic stress cases after officer involved shootings. I hoped Quinn would schedule herself an appointment with Loretta as well.

At least Paul was physically unharmed. That was something. I left him with Sam long enough to move my car to a legal parking space and retrieve the heavy beach towel, which I brought back and wrapped around Paul's shoulders, greasepaint side out.

When the police had taken everyone's statement, I drove Paul home. I'd considered taking him to the hospital, but I figured I could treat shock as well as most doctors, and he really wanted to go home.

I helped him out of his bloody clothes and stood him in a hot shower. I bagged the clothes for Quinn, in case they were needed as evidence. While Paul was in the shower, I called SFO and told them he wouldn't be coming in to work that night. Then I heated chicken soup from a can and grilled a tuna sandwich with Tillamook cheddar.

When Paul came out of the shower, I put the soup and sandwich in front of him and insisted that he eat. He finished half of the sandwich and most of the soup. Then I gave him a double shot of brandy and poured one for myself.

We talked for three hours, about Fragoso and how he'd lost his mind to the grief and anger, about Paul's co-workers who had died by Fragoso's hand, and finally about Paul's wife, who had left him.

I told him about Drew, my ex, and his triplets, and I told him about Cher getting a divorce. I had thought about setting the two of them up later when Cher's divorce was final, but Paul needed something to cling to right now, so I took the risk and offered him Cher. He lit up like a Christmas tree. He stopped shaking for the first time since the shooting and said, "You think she would go out with me?"

"You'll never know if you don't ask."

He looked at me with a mixture of hope and fear in his eyes. "I guess you're right," he said. "Okay. I'll ask her out after she's divorced."

"I'm not that patient. Besides, she's going to need company *during* the divorce. She'll need a friend she can lean on and who can help her deal with all her self-doubts. You're good at that."

I had their whole future planned out in my head.

# CHAPTER 24

THE WEEKEND BEFORE HALLOWEEN I hosted a dock party to celebrate Elizabeth and Jack's engagement. Much to my relief, while Elizabeth had accepted Jack's proposal, she'd informed me that it would take at least a year to plan the wedding of her dreams, and in the meantime she intended to continue living on her trawler. My apprehension regarding her decision to marry Jack had melted when she told me how he'd proposed, in Gaelic. While down on one knee, holding the engagement ring nestled in a black velvet box, he'd said, "Is breá liom tú, Elizabeth. Déan dom an fear happiest ar fud an domhain, agus a aontú a bheith ar mo bhean chéile."

I didn't understand Gaelic, but Elizabeth was happy to translate for me.

The dock party attendees included Cher,

Paul, Elizabeth and Jack, of course, Lily (a
marina neighbor who grew up with Elizabeth),
Sam, Rebecca, and her boss David Ralston.
They all arrived between 1:30 and 2:00. I'd
borrowed a banquet table from the marina
management office and set out a buffet on the
wide cement dock.

Sam and I had a date to go sailing the
following week and he spent some time looking
over the boat, when he wasn't busy chastising
me for the risks I'd taken in the park.

Bill barbecued steak and salmon, and
Jack had brought potato salad and pumpkin
bread made by his cook and housekeeper,
Ilsa Richter.

Elizabeth was wearing her engagement
ring: a two-carat marquis-cut diamond flanked
by a pair of half-carat emerald baguettes set in
platinum. I couldn't help staring at the ring,
and at Elizabeth. She looked so happy.

Paul and Cher sat on the deck of my boat
drinking wine coolers and talking about Paul's
recent ordeal. He'd been to see Loretta twice
in the last week, and said she was helping him
deal with the panic attacks. When I passed by
carrying trays of food to the table I overheard
Paul talking openly about how terrified he
had been. Cher was holding his hand between
both of hers, comforting him.

Back at the buffet table I watched Rebecca admiring Elizabeth's engagement ring. David hovered behind her, his eyes filled with longing. Rebecca and I had bonded over surveillance videos of Wallace, the perv, watching her and taking snapshots of her with his telephoto lens. I had changed my mind about her friendship potential, even though she was ridiculously perfect.

"Rebecca," I said, "would you help me carry the watermelon down from my car?"

She turned to look at me, shrugged, and said, "Sure."

I think my desire to play matchmaker comes from watching too many romantic comedies when I was a kid. I put my arm around her shoulders as we walked up to shore and asked, "What's the deal with David?"

"What do you mean?"

"Well, he's clearly in love with you. How do you feel about him?"

"He's not in love with me. He's never even made a pass at me."

"He's shy. And you didn't answer my question."

"I'm *crazy* about him!" She sounded angry.

"So what's the problem?"

"You'll laugh," she said more quietly. I raised an eyebrow. "He's so sweet and gentle," she averted her eyes, too embarrassed to look at me when she said, "I'm afraid he might be a disappointment in bed."

"I see. So, tell me how you feel when he plays the piano."

She stared at me for a long moment, and I watched as recognition kicked in.

"Oh, my God," she finally said. "I am such an idiot. I've been working for that man for two years and I've wanted him since the day I met him."

Am I good or what?

Of course there was no watermelon in my car. When we arrived back at the party Rebecca walked right up to David and kissed him.

He blushed happily. "What was that for?" he asked.

"I'll tell you later," she said, and winked at me.

I stood near the buffet table and peered up at Paul and Cher. Buddy had insinuated himself between them, lying on the bench seat with his forepaws in Paul's lap. Cher was laughing at something Paul had said and they were both petting the dog. I'd decided to keep Buddy for myself and had taken down all the pictures of him that I'd posted around the marina.

Bill set a platter of steaming beef and

salmon on the table and leaned in close to me. "I just got a call on that sex offender homicide," he whispered. "I need to go into the office. Sorry."

He gave me a quick kiss before removing his chef's apron and striding up the dock. Little did I know how much that particular case was going to change my life in the coming months.

As I watched Bill hurry away I noticed one of my neighbors storming down the dock. Sarah is in her mid-fifties, about five-five and one-seventy, with short red hair and a tendency to be blunt. She looked upset as she moved toward me.

"Nikki," she said. "I hate to interrupt the party, but I need your help."

I breathed a sigh of relief. Sarah has been known to cause a scene about parties on the docks when she's not invited.

"What's up?" I asked, escorting her aboard the boat and down into the galley so as not to disturb my guests.

"It's Larry," she said. "He's *missing!*" And with that, she burst into tears.

Larry is Sarah's prize-winning Persian cat. He's also a well-known busybody. One day when I'd left my hatch and pilothouse doors open because of the heat, I came home and caught Larry snooping around my main salon.

He flew past me and up the companionway so fast that by the time I made it up the steps he was already halfway down the dock. I'd heard similar stories from my neighbors.

I sat Sarah down at the galley counter, handed her a box of tissues, and poured her a shot of Jameson's.

"When did you see him last?" I asked.

~THE END~

# About the Author

Nancy Skopin is a native of California, and currently lives on the Oregon coast with her husband and their dogs.

While researching her mystery series she spent two years working for a private investigator learning the intricacies of the business. She also worked closely with a police detective who became both a consultant and a friend. For thirteen years, she lived aboard her yacht in the San Francisco Bay Area, as does her central character, Nicoli Hunter.

If you'd like to be notified when new
Nikki Hunter mysteries come out, e-mail
me at: NikkiMaxineHunter@gmail.com

Made in the USA
Coppell, TX
28 December 2020

47230454R00156